HEARTSIDE BAY

Winter Wonderland

CATHY COLE

SCHOLASTIC

To our lovely Grace, you are our sunshine.
Mum, David, Ellie, Emily and Andrew.

Scholastic Children's Books
An imprint of Scholastic Ltd
Euston House, 24 Eversholt Street, London, NW1 1DB, UK
Registered office: Westfield Road, Southam, Warwickshire, CV47 0RA
SCHOLASTIC and associated logos are trademarks and/or
registered trademarks of Scholastic Inc.

First published in the UK by Scholastic Ltd, 2014

Text copyright © Scholastic Ltd, 2014

ISBN 978 1407 145525

A CIP catalogue record for this book
is available from the British Library.

Printed by CPI Group (UK) Ltd, Croydon, CR0 4YY
Papers used by Scholastic Children's Books are made
from wood grown in sustainable forests.

1 3 5 7 9 10 8 6 4 2

www.scholastic.co.uk

Forever love and thanks
to Lucy Courtenay and Sara Grant

ONE

Eve Somerstown knew someone was watching her. It was hard to explain how she knew, but she did. The air had changed imperceptibly, thickening in some way.

Eve was striking and she knew it. She was tall and slim with glossy auburn hair and bright steel-grey eyes, and she was used to people looking at her. She adjusted her stride a little, pulling her shoulders back and flipping her hair away from her face to present herself in the best possible light. She might have been wearing a hideous black-and-red school uniform, but she still looked stylish. *Once the Queen of Heartside Bay, always the Queen of Heartside Bay*, she thought with some satisfaction.

The curving street that led down the hill into town

shimmered and faded to nothing. In its place Eve imagined a long red carpet, cheering crowds penned back with a silken purple rope, paparazzi firing their cameras at her. She raised her chin a little higher, and elongated her stride. More people turned their heads to watch her progress. Her life may have been ripped apart and shaken all over the place in the past few months, but she still had what it took to turn heads.

"Hi, gorgeous."

The red carpet faded and Heartside Bay came sharply back into view again. Eve's heart sank as she saw who had greeted her. Tristan de Vere. "Oh," she said, cuttingly. "It's you."

"There's no need to sound so excited," Tristan grinned.

He had styled his hair to perfection this morning. *No change there then*, Eve thought with considerable dislike. Tristan had been at Heartside High for precisely one week. One week too long, in Eve's opinion.

"Did you hear about the football then?" he asked casually as they walked side by side down the street towards school.

Eve kept her face blank. She wouldn't give Tristan

the satisfaction of knowing that she and her friends had been talking about little else all weekend. She pictured her friend Ollie's miserable face as they had all sat commiserating with him in the Heartbeat Café on Saturday evening, and hated Tristan a little bit more. "I don't follow football," she said carelessly. "It's a boring game, played by boring people."

Tristan examined his perfectly trimmed fingernails. "Not the way I play it. As Ollie Wright found out on Saturday. He'll be on the bench for a while, I'm sorry to say." He reconsidered. "Actually, I'm not sorry at all."

"Is there no end to your talents?" Eve said sarcastically.

He smirked. "When you've got it, you've got it."

Urgh! Eve wanted to *scream*. Who did this guy think he was? *The hottest news in town*, said the little voice in her head. Tristan de Vere was all anyone seemed to be talking about. She had lost count of the number of girls who were hanging around the school gates at the end of the day, trying to catch the hot new boy's attention. He had money, good looks, great clothes, charm – when he wanted to use it. All the things that she used to have, back in the days when she was the person everyone wanted to know. Before her father had ruined everything and ended up in jail.

Eve snapped her mind shut. She didn't want to think about her father today.

"Loving the outfit," Tristan said, sliding his eyes teasingly up and down Eve's blazer. "Don't tell me. Chanel? D&G? It fits you like a glove."

"Gloves go on your hands," Eve said sweetly. "Didn't anyone ever tell you that?"

Tristan looked unconcerned by the sarcasm in her voice. "You still look hot in it. You'd look hot in anything. I bet you're scorching in a bikini."

Now Eve was seriously grossed out. "It's the twenty-first century, not 1987," she snapped. "Where do you get off making remarks like that?"

"Hey," said Tristan, raising his hands. "It's a compliment! Girls are so touchy about compliments these days."

It hadn't sounded like a compliment to Eve. It had sounded like a sleazy chat-up line, and she'd heard plenty of those. For one brief moment, she felt like laughing. Tristan obviously didn't know she was gay.

You want to play? she thought, smiling privately to

herself. *Fine. I'll play.* Keep your friends close and your enemies closer – wasn't that what people said?

She glanced up at Tristan through her long dark eyelashes, a move she hadn't used in a while. Pretty much since she'd started dating Becca, now she came to think about it. "Sorry," she said, with a coy smile. "I guess I can take a compliment."

Tristan's smile grew broader. "Of course you can, beautiful. Especially when it's a compliment from me. I haven't been throwing them around much lately. Nothing much to compliment around here, is there?"

He raised his eyebrows pointedly at the peeling paint on the shop windows and the tattered, sun-bleached bunting that was hung over their heads across the High Street.

"Oh, I don't know," said Eve, flicking him another loaded glance. "I can think of something."

Tristan thrust out his chest. "Keep looking, sweetheart. I'm the best around."

Boys were so predictable, Eve thought with a sigh. "There must be something else you like about Heartside Bay," she said.

"You're joking," he snorted. "The shops stink. The

social life is dire. There's no cinema, no golf course. That thing you call a marina is just a posh fishing harbour." More kids surged into their path, a river of black-and-red blazers. Tristan wrinkled his nose, adding: "And don't you just love the smell of polyester in the morning?"

Eve had never particularly loved her quirky town. The houses were mostly shabby, no one drove decent cars, and he was right about the shops. But, as she listened to his list of sneering complaints, she found herself wanting to defend it. He was so *judgemental*. Was it possible to hate this guy even more than she already did? But she covered her irritation with a smile and a throaty laugh that suggested agreement.

"Listen," Tristan said, "we should get together some time."

"What do you mean?" Eve asked innocently.

"You and me. On a date. You're the most beautiful girl in school and I'm the most attractive guy. We're meant to be together. It's destiny."

The old Eve would have jumped at the offer, She realized with a jolt of discomfort. It was scary how much of her old self she recognized in this brash newcomer. Now ... all she could hear was the insincerity in Tristan's voice, the overbearing confidence. She thought of Becca with her big laugh and her chestnut hair and her open, freckled face. Still. . . She felt a rush of excitement that she hadn't felt in a long time. Flirting was pretty fun, even though she had no intention of dating the guy.

"You'll have to try harder than that," she said with a toss of her head.

He laughed. "This town is a dump, but my house isn't so bad. I have a really great room. You should come up and see it this afternoon."

And he had the gall to wink. The guy's confidence beggared belief. Did he really think it was that easy? Reaching out, Eve dabbed him on the end of his perfect nose, laughing privately to herself.

"Maybe some other day. I have plans," she purred.

Tristan was undaunted. "The address is 23 Osborn Road. In case you change your mind."

Eve staggered in shock.

"Hey," he said, catching her by the elbow. "I know I'm pretty knockout, but I don't usually send girls flying."

Eve snatched her arm back. The mention of her old address had thrown her completely. *I live at 23 Osborn Road,* she wanted to snarl. *Not you.* She could picture the house as it had been before her father's arrest, full of beautiful things. . . Her room with its marble en-suite bathroom – her walk-in wardrobe, the chandelier in the hall. . . For one wild moment, Eve felt as if she had slipped into a parallel world where she had never existed. Tristan had replaced her in Heartside Bay, in every single way. Him and his entire family.

Eve looked dumbly into his mocking black eyes, taking in his sickly smile, smelling his expensive cologne. In that moment, she realized just how far she had fallen. She had to find her way back to the top again. Somehow.

TWO

"So," Tristan prompted, when Eve didn't say anything. "Do we have a date?"

Eve's mind was still whirling with memories. She mustered a smile from somewhere, wondering what she was going to say. There was no way she was going to go on a date with Tristan de Vere. Part of her wanted to tell him as much. Tell him that she wouldn't be caught dead with a slimeball like him. The rest of her felt cautious. Tristan de Vere would make a useful friend – and a dangerous enemy. She knew his type. She had been just like him, once.

Her phone started vibrating with a call. Eve had never felt so relieved.

"This is going to have to wait for another time,"

she said. Summoning her courage, she leaned in to kiss Tristan on the cheek.

Tristan tried to kiss her properly, moving his lips swiftly towards hers. Eve twisted her head away just in time, and his mouth met her ear.

"See you," she said, backing away.

"You'll be my date to my party on Friday, right?" Tristan called, but Eve had already swerved away into the black-and-red sea of school uniforms, blending in with the crowd, pulling her phone from her bag as she walked.

Her stomach disappeared as she stared at the screen. Only one person she knew called from an unavailable number. *I can't talk to him*, she thought at once. *Not now. Not yet.* What was she supposed to say, anyway? *Hi, Daddy, you ruined my life. I hope I never see you again?*

Eve dismissed the call with a jab of her thumb. She walked a little faster, thrusting the phone back into her bag. She hoped Tristan wouldn't catch her up and try to pick up where he left off. She was even less in the mood for his slimy approaches now.

Despite herself, Eve could hear her father's voice

in her head. He had called her his princess, his Evie. She felt a sudden rush of sadness. She couldn't deny it, however hard she tried. She missed her dad. She hadn't seen him since he'd been sent to prison.

I miss the person I thought he was, she reminded herself, pursing her lips. *I don't miss the criminal that he became.*

Her father had screwed up her whole existence. Her family had been destitute for a while, evicted from their home, all because of his stupidity and his greed. If Eve had learned one thing from the horrifying experiences of the past few months, it was that money was worthless without honesty and integrity. Two qualities her father lacked.

Her phone buzzed once softly from deep inside her bag, a sad little indication of a voicemail message. Eve clenched her fists. She wouldn't check the phone. She refused to dial into voicemail just to hear her father's lying voice. Keeping her head bowed and her hands thrust deep into her blazer pockets, Eve walked on. The school steps couldn't come fast enough.

"Oh!" Eve gasped, colliding with someone and almost losing her footing. "I'm sorry, I wasn't—"

"Looking where you were going?" Lila Murray enquired, her blue eyes bright with amusement as she steadied Eve with both hands. "I noticed."

"Lila!" she gasped, pulling her surprised friend into a tight hug. "I can't tell you how pleased I am to see a friendly face! I have had the *worst* morning."

Lila returned the hug, wrapping her arms around Eve's shoulders. "Whoa, hugs before school? What's up?"

Eve wanted to cry at the sudden concern in her friend's voice. She squeezed Lila more tightly than ever. "Tristan," she groaned into Lila's shoulder.

"What's he done now?"

Eve linked arms with Lila as they took the school steps together. "He's living in my old house," she said miserably. "He just asked me out and then he said his address, and the whole world tipped sideways. He said something about a party on Friday too, at my place. I mean, his place. Urgh, I'm in such a muddle—"

Lila stopped dead, pulling Eve back with her. "He asked you to be his date to the party?" she said incredulously.

"I don't think I—" Eve stopped and frowned at her friend. "Wait. You know about the party?"

Lila rolled her eyes. "*Everyone* knows about the party."

"Everyone except me, apparently," Eve said tersely. She tried not to think about the times when she was the one throwing the parties.

"Well, yes, big deal, he's having a party on Friday," Lila said with a shrug. "You'll probably get an invitation today. Backtracking here. He asked you *out*? What did you say? Did you tell him to take a running jump? I would have paid good money to see that."

Eve smiled faintly. "Let's just say, I left him hanging."

"Dangling from a cliff from one arm," Lila said gleefully. "Can I be the one to stamp on his fingers?" And she exploded into giggles.

This time, Eve did laugh. Her friend's humour was infectious.

"I can't believe he asked you out!" Lila said when she stopped laughing to draw breath. "But it's nothing to be miserable about. He may be an idiot, but he's also extremely hot. So, are you going out with him?"

Eve raised her eyebrows. "I'm already going out with Becca, in case you'd forgotten. I don't date boys any more."

"*I* know that. But does he?"

Eve shook her head.

"Don't you think you should tell him?"

Now it was Eve's turn to frown. "Why should I?"

"Don't string him along, Eve," Lila warned. "Tristan de Vere doesn't look like the type of guy you want to get on the wrong side of."

Eve had a feeling Lila was right. She changed the subject.

"I also had a call," she said carefully. She needed to tell someone. She had to sort out how she was feeling. She hated feeling so out of control. "From my dad."

Lila made a hissing sound through her teeth. "You did? How did he sound?"

"I didn't talk to him," Eve said after a moment. *I couldn't*, she thought unhappily.

"You have to talk to him some time, Eve. Whatever he's done, he's still your dad."

Eve glared. She may have wanted advice, but that didn't make it any easier to hear. "I don't have to talk to him if I don't want to," she snapped. "He's my father, Lila. I make the decisions."

Lila squeezed her shoulder. "You have to do what you think is best. But in my opinion, you seem really freaked out by this. Don't you want to fix that? You could see him, at least. Even if you can't forgive him yet."

Eve bit her lip and stayed silent.

Lila checked her watch. "Oops, better go. I've been late three times already this term and we've only had five days of school. See you later."

She took the rest of the steps two at a time, leaving Eve behind. Eve thought about the voicemail message winking silently in her bag. She moved a little apart from the main flow of people and took out her phone.

Her father's voice sounded croaky with tiredness and emotion. "Evie, honey, I wish you would talk to me. Come and visit me, please. I have so much to make up for. Give me a chance, princess. I. . ." His voice caught, wobbled, then moved on. "It's lonely in here. Your mother and sister won't come. You're the only one I have left, Evie."

In the background Eve could hear muffled clangs

and yells, the sounds of a prison corridor. She pictured her father in a queue, a line of impatient men behind him waiting to use the phone. It was a lonely image.

Eve knew her father was right about her mother and Chloe. They wouldn't dirty the soles of their designer shoes on the floor of a prison. *You're the only one I have left. . .*

I have to visit him, she thought wearily. *Before all this happened, he was the best father in the world.* She had to give him a chance. Didn't she?

THREE

Eve climbed warily off the bus and gazed around.
This wasn't a part of town she'd ever visited before.
Not hard to see why, she thought dryly, taking in the
scruffy buildings and the litter blowing along the street.

It had taken a lot of persuading to allow this visit to
happen at all.

"I don't want you there," her mum had said shrilly
when Eve had first raised the subject of visiting her
father. "You could pick up something nasty. I won't
have Chloe infected."

Eve had pleaded, sulked, cajoled. She had flattered
her mother, made her cups of tea, told her how young
she was looking. And eventually she had agreed, and
signed the consent form.

Eve had packed something inconspicuous to wear in her school bag that morning, something she could change into straight after school and that would, hopefully, blend in with the other visitors to Oakham Open Prison. She adjusted her hat self-consciously, and pulled her coat collar up a little. Even this far out of the centre of town, you never knew who you might see.

The bus ride had been longer than expected, and Eve had found herself checking her watch anxiously. Visiting hours were strict. If she was late, something told her that all the charm in the world wouldn't persuade the guards to let her see her father.

The signs to the prison were clearly marked on the roadside. Even if Eve hadn't spotted them, the only people who had ridden the bus this far were obviously here for the same reason as her. All she had to do was follow them. It was a thought that made her feel very strange. She looked surreptitiously at the other people walking down the street with her – blank, tired faces, many of them, some with children in buggies and some alone. Eve couldn't bring herself to start a conversation with anyone. She felt scared, and very alone.

She'd never visited a prison before. All she could

picture were the gloomy, echoing prisons of movies and TV shows – prisoners in orange boiler suits, bars, shiny green walls. So Oakham Open Prison, when she reached it after a brief five-minute trudge, came as a surprise.

The building was modern, with gleaming windows and chrome doors. There was a central reception area with cheerful potted plants, and views of green hills and fields through the windows. There wasn't a barred door or a padlock to be seen. The men imprisoned here were white-collar criminals, not considered a threat to society.

It began to feel more prison-like as Eve made her way slowly through security.

"Visiting order?" said the lady at the desk, in a brisk voice.

Eve fumbled clumsily in her bag and handed over the visiting order, along with her mother's consent form. Thank goodness she was sixteen now, or she wouldn't have been allowed to come unaccompanied.

The receptionist nodded at Eve's school bag. "You'll need to put that in a locker before you go through. Do you have a pound coin?"

Eve clutched her bag tightly to her chest. "What? Why?"

"Visitors can't take personal belongings inside."

Someone laughed in the line behind her. *They're probably laughing at me*, Eve thought. *The stupid posh girl who doesn't know prison rules.*

Eve's identification was checked and her visiting order stamped. Across the reception area, she saw a row of blue lockers, where she stowed her bag before joining another queue. Life in prison was a little like school, she reflected. Rules, queues, lockers—

She felt someone's hands on her body and recoiled. "Get off!" she snapped.

The prison officer looked impassive. "Standard procedure, miss. Raise your arms for me."

Eve flushed to the roots of her hair, but did as the guard told her. The woman's hands patted her up and down, along her arms and down her legs. It was like something out of a bad dream, the way the guards were looking at her, the other people whispering about her. . . It was all she could do not to bolt for the doors and run back into the littered street to hurl herself on a bus home again.

"All set." The guard patted her on the shoulder. "In you go."

Eve gathered her scattered wits. *You've made it this far. You can't cave now*, she thought. And she went into the visitors' room.

A thin, bearded man in the corner half-stood from a black plastic chair, his hand raised in her direction. Automatically, she looked behind her. Then, realization dawning, she looked back at the bearded man again. *Really* looked.

"Daddy?" she heard herself say.

Henry Somerstown had lost at least two stone. His hair was longer. And the beard. . . She'd never seen her father with so much facial hair before. It didn't suit him.

"Evie, baby! It's so good to see you!"

The bearded man wrapped his arms around her and hugged her. Dazed and not knowing how to react, Eve held herself stiffly until a guard stepped in and separated them.

"No kissing, long embraces, physical contact," said the guard in a bored voice. It was plain that he'd said it a hundred times before.

Eve managed to unstick her limbs and sit, a little unsteadily, in the chair her father was indicating.

"Princess!" Henry Somerstown sounded choked. "You are a breath of fresh air, do you know that? Your hair's different. What did you do to it?"

Forgot to brush it, probably, Eve thought.

"Tell me your news! How's school? Friends?"

Eve found her voice. "Fine," she said awkwardly. "What about you?"

Her father waved his arm in a gesture Eve remembered him using whenever they flew on the private jet he had used for his business. "All the better for seeing my princess. Five-star accommodation in here, Evie. You know me, only the best."

At what cost? Eve thought. She fiddled with her skirt as her father smiled. What did he want her to say next? How was she supposed to talk to this liar who happened to be her father? This fraudster who had ruined everything, this cheat who had wrecked people's lives?

"How's your mother?" he prompted.

"Fine."

"Chloe? I expect she's grown."

"She's fine too." *Different vocabulary needed*, Eve thought a little haphazardly. She made herself look at her father. His eyes were tired and his face was too thin. She wanted to tell him to stop pretending. Nothing was fine. Nothing was five-star. There were potted plants in reception, but this was still jail. Despite herself, her eyes pricked with tears.

"None of that, Evie," her father said, suddenly sounding sharp. "I don't need pity. Not from you, not from anyone."

Eve felt as if she'd been slapped. Her father never spoke to her like that. Not the father she knew, anyway. "I wasn't. . . I didn't—"

Her father patted her hand awkwardly. "Hey, princess, ignore me. I've been in here too long. Tell me your news. Any good parties lately? Your parties were always the best."

When we had the money to spend on them. "I don't have parties any more," said Eve, a little bleakly.

Her father changed the subject. "Have you come across the de Veres yet? They have a boy around your age. He must have started at Heartside High by now."

Eve's mouth fell open. How did her father know about Tristan de Vere?

Her father saw her astonishment. He tapped his nose with a flash of his old charm. "I'm not totally out of the loop in here, Evie. I know Annie de Vere has taken over the shopping centre project. We used to run across each other from time to time, at business functions and that kind of thing." He looked sad for a moment. "What's the boy like, then?"

"I don't really know him yet." *But what I've seen doesn't bode well*, Eve thought. This was such a strange conversation. She found herself wishing she hadn't come to the prison at all.

Her father held her hands tightly and looked at her with a kind of desperation. "We'll get it all back again when I'm out, princess. I promise you. Everything will be the same, you'll see. A nice house, all the clothes and parties you want. There are a couple of schemes I'm working on in here that could see us right—"

Eve had heard enough. She pulled her hands away. "You don't get it yet, do you Daddy?" she said. "You don't understand what you've done at all. Our lives will never be the same. Never. All the promises in the world can't change that!"

Her father looked desperate as Eve rose from her chair. He stood too. "I'll make it up to you," he said. "You, Chloe, your mother. . . I'll fix this, Evie, I promise you—"

"Promises!" Eve spat. "Your promises mean nothing. I learned that months ago, when I had nothing to eat and nowhere to live and everyone hated me. Get away from me, don't touch me. . ." He was reaching for her, but she was pushing him away, and guards were running towards them, their mouths pressed to walkie-talkies, and everywhere people were looking— "I shouldn't have come here, I should have listened to Mummy when she told me not to come, get off me, I hate you. . . I'll never forgive you. . . *Never*!"

FOUR

"I can't do this."

Eve felt as if she'd been saying this a lot lately. Ever since her disastrous prison visit, and the shouting, and the bus ride home in a flood of tears, everything that had previously been easy now felt so *hard*. Like she was swimming against the tide, trying to reach the shore.

"*You* can't do this?" Becca wailed in horror. "What about *me*? You used to throw grand parties all the time, the way you tell it. The last time I went to a party like this, I was eight years old!"

Eve looked again at the familiar front of her old house. Tristan had rigged up a light system that made the steps leading to the front door look as if they were cascading like a tropical waterfall. Two girls in shimmering sparkly dresses were giggling together by the door, clutching their invitations. Boys were pretending to swim their way up the steps to make their dates laugh. There was a hollow feeling in Eve's stomach as she remembered all the parties she had thrown in the past. The lights, the music, the waiters in tuxedos. The pale blue dress she was wearing tonight was over a year old and her shoes were a little scuffed. *Shoes get trodden on, big deal,* she'd thought when getting ready earlier that evening. Things had changed a lot since the days when it had been her at the top of those steps, welcoming her guests with a drink and a flirtatious smile. When a scuffed shoe had spelled the end of the world.

"I hate my dress, Eve," Becca groaned, pulling Eve back into the moment. "I should never have worn it. You should have talked me out of it, I look like a massive bin liner."

Eve made an effort to think about her girlfriend. It helped distract her from the weirdness. "You look gorgeous," she said, stroking Becca's chestnut hair away from her face. "An expert did your eye make-up, right?"

Becca refused to be mollified. "*You* did it, you twonk. And I still think one eye looks bigger than the other. I didn't know you were wearing that blue dress tonight."

"If you'd charged your phone when you were at work, I could have told you," Eve said. Becca had taken a job at an ice-cream parlour down by the beach, not far from her grandmother's holiday cottage where she was staying. The cottage had no electricity or running water, as Eve had found out not so long ago when she had run away after her father had been arrested.

Becca rolled her eyes. "It's a beach shack. They only have one plug and they use it for the freezer. I can hardly unplug that to charge my phone, can I? I'd be out of a job faster than you could say 'melted mint choc chip'."

Eve didn't want a fight. She hadn't seen her girlfriend in over a week, thanks to Becca's job and her being back at school. So she smiled and kissed Becca and told her again how gorgeous she was looking until her girlfriend thawed and started smiling again.

Eve spotted what looked like Josh's hat deep in the

throng at the top of the steps. Remembering that her friends would be here tonight, supporting her through the strangeness, gave her a boost of confidence. She could do anything with them around her, even endure a party in her old house hosted by Mr Slime.

"Time to dive in," she said, and towed Becca up the steps.

The band was playing something with a heavy beat from up on the landing above the main hall. Eve took a deep breath as she gazed at the familiar space, the chandelier and the marble floor. There was a new hall table, a great big gilded thing that wouldn't have looked out of place in a palace. *Hold it together,* she thought.

"Nice place," Becca remarked, gazing around. "Terrible furniture."

Eve giggled, feeling a little better. "Mum made this look a lot more tasteful. She changed the decor every time she got bored with it, which was approximately every six months. The chandelier's the same, though. Lila, hey!"

Lila looked fantastic, in a short bronze-coloured dress that brought out the highlights in her long dark hair. Dangly gold earrings and gold gladiator sandals completed the picture. "I thought I'd go a bit Greek," she giggled, exchanging kisses. "I always loved that dress on you, Eve. Becca, you look amazing!"

"Is Josh here?" asked Eve, looking around the crowded room. "I thought I saw his hat."

"Urgh, that hat," Lila groaned. "I keep trying to make him throw it away, but he's stupidly attached to it. A straw hat and a tux? Puhlease. I'm going to pretend he's not my date if he keeps wearing it. Look, there's Rhi. And Polly too!"

Polly's boyfriend Ollie and Josh were at the bar fetching drinks. As everyone came together, laughing and teasing and exclaiming over each other's outfits, Eve felt better. Parties were about friends, after all. It amazed her that she'd never realized that before.

The music changed. Across the room, Eve could see Tristan's tall dark head in the heart of a crowd, holding court. Suddenly she wanted to be somewhere else.

"Come on," she said, taking Becca's hand. "Let me give you the grand tour."

The crowds thinned as they left the main hall. Eve showed Becca the large kitchen with its now-black kitchen units, the snug and the formal dining room.

"What's in there?" Becca said as Eve pulled her past a closed door.

"My dad's study," Eve said shortly. She had no wish to enter that room. It held too many painful memories. "Come on, we can cut back this way to the hall—"

"Two gorgeous ladies for the price of one!"

Eve stopped in dismay. Tristan de Vere had appeared from somewhere, smiling at her with his big white teeth.

"Everyone's been wondering when my date was going to show up. Come on, you're missing the fun."

Without giving Eve a chance to say a word, Tristan started guiding her through the crowds to where the hum of the band was loudest. Eve dug in her heels, casting an agonized glance over her shoulder to where Becca seemed to have been turned to stone.

"Tristan," she tried, "stop – this is my friend Becca – *Tristan*—"

Tristan continued moving towards the main hall, his arm firmly around Eve's waist. "Brought a friend, did you?" he said, turning round to wink at Becca.

Becca shot him such a poisonous look that Eve was surprised he didn't turn into a puddle of green slime on the spot.

"Who," said Becca loudly, "is this?"

"This isn't what it looks like, Bec," Eve tried to say, but the noise in the hall was too loud and the music was thumping through her head. She turned back to Tristan again, horrified by the turn of events, trying her best to make herself understood.

"Make room for my beautiful date!" Tristan called, smiling left and right at the assembled guests. Several girls glared daggers in Eve's direction. It would have been funny if it wasn't so awful. *What must Becca be thinking?* Eve wondered wildly.

"I'm not your date, Tristan," she tried to say. "I'm here with Becca."

He seemed to hear her this time. "Two for the price of one, is it?" he said, raising his eyebrows and laughing. "Suits me just fine. Who's going first?"

"Take your hands off my girlfriend," said Becca coldly.

Things were starting to spiral away from Eve's control. Tristan was calling for drinks, draping his arm around Eve's shoulder and making it clear that she was with him – only she wasn't with him at all. . .

"Take your hands," Becca repeated more loudly, "OFF MY GIRLFRIEND."

"Feisty one, aren't you?" Tristan drawled, still failing to understand. "Like the dress, by the way. And I could drown in those big eyes of yours."

"Go right ahead," Becca snarled.

Eve knew she had to explain before things got completely out of hand. "Tristan, please – can we talk somewhere a bit quieter?"

Tristan spread his arms before the watching crowd. Eve registered her friends watching, wide-eyed. "This is as quiet as it gets at a de Vere party, babes."

He doesn't get it, Eve thought helplessly. Why would he? How could she make him understand? She remembered what Lila had said, about not making an enemy of Tristan de Vere. . . Why hadn't she been straight with him from the start?

Becca solved the problem. Pushing Tristan out of the way, she put her arms around Eve and planted a long and passionate kiss on her lips. There was an audible gasp from the assembled crowd. Silent at last,

Tristan gaped in astonishment.

"Did the penny drop yet?" Becca asked as she came up for air. "Eve is my girlfriend. Not a girl who's a friend. *Girlfriend*. We date. We kiss. We hold hands."

Eve wanted to melt into the floor with embarrassment. She wasn't used to feeling this way. Nor, it seemed, was Tristan. He was lost for words before. A flush of colour was stealing up his cheeks. Several people in the crowd were laughing, pointing. *I'm sorry,* she wanted to say, *but you just weren't listening. . .*

"Oh my God," Tristan said at last, recovering his poise. "Are you two some kind of circus act?"

"Don't speak to our friends like that!" Ollie had pushed her way through the crowd, his normally cheerful eyes sparking with rage. Eve wanted to hug him for his loyalty.

Tristan sneered. "Turned you down, did they?"

Polly moved beside Ollie, putting her hand on his arm to restrain him. "This is a party," she pleaded. "This is all just a simple misunderstanding. You—"

"You're the one whose mum is dating the history teacher, aren't you?" said Tristan with a laugh. "Is there some kind of lesbian virus around here? Look at you people. You're losers, with weird gay friends."

Rhi's cheeks had a heightened colour that told Eve exactly how furious she was. "Eve, Becca," she said. "Any time you want to leave, we're right behind you."

Tristan focused on Lila, who had been watching with her mouth open in shock. "They can go," he said dismissively. "I hope you stay, though, babe. You're way too pretty to be gay. Maybe you could be my date instead?"

"In your dreams," Lila smirked.

With a sinking heart, Eve could hear flirtation in her friend's voice. *He may be an idiot, but he's also extremely hot. . .* Despite Tristan's cruelty, it looked as if Lila was in the Tristan fan club too.

There was a sudden flash of fists. Josh had come barrelling out of the crowd, throwing punches in Tristan's direction. "That's my girlfriend you're chatting up," he snarled.

Lila snapped out of her Tristan trance. "Josh," she gasped, rushing forward, "no!"

Eve found herself in the thick of the yelling crowd, helping Lila and Becca and Polly and Ollie separate Josh and Tristan before things turned nasty. Lila yanked Josh backwards so hard he almost fell backwards and lost his hat.

"Time to go, I think," Eve panted.

Becca tightened her grip on Eve's hand. She looked pale but composed. "Right behind you," she said.

"You can keep your stupid party, posh boy," Ollie snarled, his arms around Polly and Rhi. "We're out of here."

And the whole gang left amid a roar of cheers and clapping.

FIVE

Eve and her friends ran down the waterfall steps and out of Tristan's gate, laughing with the shock and exhilaration of what had just happened.

"I can't believe he said those things to you!" Rhi gasped as Becca muttered furiously under her breath. "How ignorant can you get?"

"You should have let me punch him, Lila," Josh growled. "A broken nose would have improved his face."

"And had him bring a bunch of highly paid lawyers down on your head for grievous bodily harm?" Lila enquired. "Bad idea, Joshie."

"You were a Rottweiler, man," said Ollie admiringly.

"Don't congratulate him, Ollie," Polly said with some alarm. "Josh, you can't go round hitting people all the time. . ."

"I don't hit people all the time!"

"He's just very protective of me," said Lila, slipping her arm through the crook of Josh's elbow. From the gleam in her big blue eyes, she had clearly enjoyed being the cause of the fight.

"So what are we going to do now?" Ollie said, looking around at everyone. "We're a little overdressed for a walk on the beach."

Rhi and Polly looked at each other's long, flowing dresses and high-heeled sandals and pulled faces.

"And heels and sand are a bad combination," Eve added. She had an idea. "How about we all go to the Heartbeat?"

"Can we go home and change first?" Polly asked. "I'd feel weird going to the Heartbeat dressed like this."

After her strange feelings of helplessness at the party, it felt good to take the helm again. "You look gorgeous," Eve said firmly. "We all do. It's all about making an entrance, darlings. This is the Heartbeat we're talking about. Gay or straight, black tie or trainers, everyone is welcome."

The Heartbeat Café was a good fifteen-minute walk from Tristan's house. As they walked and talked,

Eve could feel her heart rate slowing to something approaching normal again. Their table was waiting for them, in the warmth and fug of a crowded Friday night, and everyone sank gratefully into their usual chairs. Their dressy outfits attracted mild curiosity from the locals, but soon enough everyone had returned to their drinks and their conversations.

"Look," said Lila, nudging Rhi as Ollie brought over sodas. "Brody's playing."

Eve hadn't realized the blond-headed guitar player on the stage was Rhi's ex Brody Baxter. Rhi flushed. "I should have remembered he plays on Friday nights," she said.

"You don't have to know all his movements now you're not dating him any more," Ollie pointed out.

Rhi made a face at Ollie, then leaned in to Eve. "We almost have enough original songs for an album now," she confided.

"That's wonderful," Eve said warmly. Rhi and Brody were an amazing partnership, and she loved hearing them sing.

Rhi looked a little sad. "Breaking up with him was the right thing to do, wasn't it?"

"Only you know the answer to that, Rhi."

Rhi sighed. "Our musical partnership always felt stronger than our romantic one. I wish it could have worked out differently, but my gut said no."

Ollie's tummy rumbled on cue. "My gut agrees with you," he said cheerfully.

The others dissolved into laughter. Brody glanced up from his guitar at the sound. Smiling at the sight of Eve and the others, he beckoned Rhi with a twinkle in his crystal blue eyes. "You joining me up here, partner?" he said into the mic. "Rhi Wills is in the house, folks, make some noise."

"I knew Rhi hadn't dressed up for nothing," Polly said happily as Rhi stood up with a swoosh of her rainbow-hued maxi-dress and waved shyly, to loud applause, before letting Brody pull her up on to the stage beside him.

"Sing 'Sundown, Sunshine'!" someone near the back called out.

The familiar opening riff to Rhi's song broke like a wave across the crowded Heartbeat Café, the combination of Rhi and Brody's voices working their usual magic. Eve settled at her seat, Becca's hand loosely held in hers, and felt happier than she had in ages. This felt like old times, the days before Tristan de Vere had come along to ruin everything. She remembered the look on Tristan's face when Becca had kissed her. He had looked almost fearful, as if she was some kind of monster.

His problem, she thought fiercely. She looked around her close-knit group of friends, now singing along with Brody and Rhi: "Be my sundown, Sunshine, my sundown, run-up-to-sun-up Sunshine. . ."

Why do things have to change? Eve thought. *Everything is perfect, just as it is.* She didn't let herself think about potted plants, the smell of bleach or broken promises.

"My moonrise, my night skies," Rhi and Brody were singing together in gorgeous harmony. Everything was right in the world as their voices twisted together like silk ribbons and held the room spellbound. Tristan de Vere and his shallowness had no place here.

I won't let Tristan ruin what we have. I will bring him down, Eve thought in cold fury.

"My twilight, my all night, my turn-off-the-light, my Sunshine, be mine, be mine. . . My Sunshine, be mine!"

The applause was strong and warm as the song finished on its familiar rushing chords, and Brody and Rhi held hands and bowed and smiled.

"Who ordered refills?"

Rhi's dad been running the Heartbeat Café for several months now, and he always loved it when they all came in together. He set the tray of drinks down now, smiling at them all. The glasses chinked together as the applause went on drumming around them.

"Eve, you're just the person I wanted to see," Mr Wills said, setting a large glass of iced lemonade in front of her. "I have a job for you, if you're interested. It's the kind of thing that plays to your talents, I think. Although you might feel there's a conflict of interest."

Eve had helped Mr Wills organize a fashion event earlier in the summer in the old wood-panelled café, and loved every moment. *This is what I've been missing,* she thought, sitting up in excitement. *A project.* "Another fashion show?" she said hopefully.

"Not a fashion show," said Mr Wills, "but fashion could come into it if you wanted to plan it that way." He looked awkward, as if trying to work out how to explain his plan. "I wondered," he said at last, "if you'd be interested in helping the LBA – Local Business Association – promote all the local businesses in Heartside Bay?"

"That's a very broad brief, Mr Wills," said Eve in surprise. "Local businesses in Heartside include everything, from butchers to baby clothes."

"The baby-clothes place shut down a couple of weeks ago," Polly put in.

Eve was shocked. She could picture the little store in the Old Town, pretty baby things displayed in its baby blue-painted shop windows. "It did? Why?"

"It couldn't compete with the big maternity store that opened on the edge of town a few months ago," Mr Wills explained. "Local businesses get hit hard when the big guns come to town."

Something stirred in Eve's brain. "The shopping centre. . ." she said slowly.

There it was again. That strange flash of awkwardness in Mr Wills' eyes. All at once, Eve understood.

"It's fine, Mr Wills," she said, keen to put him at ease. "I know the shopping centre was Dad's idea and he started the whole development, but ever since the trial and everything . . . let's say I don't think about

43

it very favourably any more." *Particularly now the Heartside Shopping Centre development is connected to Tristan de Sneer and his family.*

Mr Wills looked relieved. "That's wonderful! Now the shopping centre development is back on track and due to open just before Christmas, a number of small-business owners, particularly around here in the Old Town, are getting worried about losing trade. They don't want to end up like Rock the Baby. So I thought perhaps you could put your mind to a solution?"

Oh, Tristan, thought Eve with a sudden flash of glee. *This could be the start of a beautiful relationship.* She couldn't think of anything she'd like to do more than rattle that particular cage.

"It's going to open before Christmas, did you say?" she said aloud. A vision stirred in her mind, of whirling snowflakes and glittering window displays, the sound of carols playing in the cobbled Old Town streets, and Eve had the answer. *It's perfect.*

"She's got that look in her eye," Lila told Josh.

"The one where we all take cover?" Josh enquired.

Eve looked around at her friends, savouring their rapt attention. "A winter festival," she said. "That's what we need. We'll call it the Heartside Bay Winter Wonderland. We'll bring the tourists down to the harbour end of the High Street, to the shops and the cafés around here. It's much prettier down at this end of town than the shiny shopping centre end. If we played up that virtue. . ."

She could almost hear silvery sleigh bells, beautiful chiming music, and feel the gentle cold of falling snow on her face. Tourists, coming to the town in throngs, wanting to buy that perfect quirky gift that only the little shops could provide. . .

Everyone started talking at once.

"I knew you'd think of something, Eve!" Mr Wills exclaimed. "Our local businesses group is going to pounce on this like an elf on a Christmas present!"

"Hot mince pies," Ollie said dreamily. "Roasting chestnuts."

"Woolly scarves that trail in the snow at our feet," Lila added.

"Snowmen!" cried the others. "Snowball fights!"

Eve took a sip of her lemonade and looked around at her friends already making eager plans. Her eyes gleamed.

Definitely one of my better ideas, she thought. *And if our festival happens to bring bad PR or take business away from Tristan's mother's shopping centre . . . so much the better.*

SIX

"Are you coming or not?" Eve demanded, the phone pressed to her ear. She felt as if she'd been waiting for Caitlin for hours.

"Darling, of course I'm coming," Caitlin said, sounding reproachful. "I wasn't up half the night discussing gorgeous Winter Wonderland ideas with you for nothing, you know. This is all going to be terribly chic, I can't wait."

Eve squinted in the bright, hot sunshine bathing the front of the Heartbeat Café. After a dull couple of weeks, summer was back with a vengeance. "Christmas isn't going to be here for a while, Cait."

"Oh darling, believe me. In the world of publicity,

every day is Christmas Day. I'll be with you in two shakes of a cashmere shawl."

Caitlin was impossible, but so gorgeous and creative and glamorous that Eve could never stay cross with her for long. She was also the first girl Eve had ever kissed, and would hold a special place in Eve's heart for ever.

Ten minutes later, Caitlin came around the corner with her arms full of files and a laptop slung across her shoulder in a chic leather case. As beautifully dressed as ever, she gave Eve a warm kiss on the cheek and chivvied her inside the café, for all the world as if it had been Eve who was late and not her.

Eve had set up a whiteboard and arranged a large table and a set of chairs in the middle of the café. As Caitlin organized the laptop and projector, Eve realized she'd arranged things the way her dad used to, for his board meetings. *I'm not thinking about Dad,* she told herself firmly.

"This better be good," Ollie yawned from his chair, clutching a frosted glass of orange juice. Polly shushed him, and made an apologetic face at Eve.

"Nine o'clock is pretty early for the weekend," Lila agreed, sitting as ever beside Josh.

"Try telling local businesses that," Eve replied briskly, which made Lila flush. "Caitlin? Do you want to start?"

The projector flicked into life, casting rainbow colours on to the whiteboard. Everyone leaned forward, scrutinizing the bright logo. It was fun, festive and Christmassy, with scribbly trees, strings of lights and a jaunty-looking robin perched on the top. It was also unmistakably Josh's style, graphic and strong.

"Did you draw that, Josh?" asked Lila in surprise.

Josh tipped his hat a little further back from his head. "I might have done," he said, and grinned at Eve.

Josh had been on the phone with Eve and Caitlin half the night, getting the logo details right.

Caitlin's presentation was filled with great ideas. They would build on Heartside Bay's reputation as the "love capital of England", and decorate the High Street accordingly. There would be music, and stalls, and food, and activities.

"We need to encourage *all* the local businesses to participate," Eve told the listeners, "not just those in the Old Town. We can encourage them to come up with mini-events and activities of their own, to coincide with the festival."

"How long is it going to run?" Rhi asked, cradling a large cup of coffee in her hands.

"A month, from mid-November right up until Christmas itself." Caitlin grinned. "Let's see the shopping centre compete with *that*. Eve darling, give everyone the flyers."

Eve handed everyone a stack of brightly coloured flyers, which had been printed with Josh's logo overnight through one of Caitlin's business contacts.

"We have the whole of today to distribute these," she said. "We're talking a massive charm offensive. Everyone needs to get out there and sell our ideas. Cait and I will join you later. It's time, darlings, to *think Christmas*."

Everyone pushed back their chairs and headed for the café doors, clutching their flyers. The light of challenge was in their eyes, Eve was satisfied to see.

"Publicity-wise, the town sells itself," said Caitlin as Mr Wills brought over coffees for them both. "It doesn't even know how pretty it is. We'll work the 'decline of the high street' angle, the press loves a story like that. One small seaside town, banding together to fight the corporate monsters."

"Do you really think the press will go for that?" Eve asked eagerly.

Caitlin nodded. "And we're talking *national* press, darling. Magazines too. If this campaign kicks off the way I'm hoping, the papers will be all over us."

Eve left Caitlin making calls and emerged into the sunshine, where she saw Lila sitting on the pavement with her face tipped towards the sun.

"Finally!" Lila announced, standing up. "The others all charged off like their shoes were on fire. I thought I'd wait for you."

"And catch a few last rays of summer," Eve observed.

Lila grinned. "That too. Come on."

They tried a local men's clothing shop first. The clothes were expensive, well-made, discreet. The last time Eve had been in here, it had been to help her father to choose a new shirt. She slammed the door on that particular memory and handed a flyer over the counter with her best smile.

51

"Hello, we're promoting a Winter Wonderland festival for local businesses in Heartside Bay, to counter the effects of the shopping centre opening this Christmas."

"You have my attention," said the shop owner, leaning forward on his elbows.

Eve explained as best she could, feeling encouraged by the way the shop owner was nodding. "The shopping centre could seriously damage the identity of our town," she said earnestly. "We want to help you attract as much business as you can."

Out of the corner of Eve's eye she saw a movement. Tristan de Vere was walking out of the curtained dressing-room at the back of the shop. Browsing the expensive watches in a glass case by the till, Lila gave a loud gasp, while Eve's stomach did a somersault. *I should have known he'd shop in this place*, she thought. How much had Tristan heard?

Tristan ignored Eve. Lila, however. . . Eve watched as her friend got the full benefit of Tristan's laser smile.

"Hi, gorgeous. What do you think of the shirt? I think it's a little tight myself." He smirked at Lila and smoothed the shirt down his lean torso. It set off his toned body beautifully. "I could use a real woman's opinion."

Was it Eve's imagination, or had he lightly stressed the word "real"? "The shopping centre will change Heartside Bay for ever," she continued firmly, keeping her eyes on the shop owner and doing her best not to notice the pretty flush rising in Lila's cheeks. "If we all work together, we can bring the rest of this town a great deal of Christmas business."

"It's, um, very nice," Lila squeaked as Tristan slowly tucked his shirt into the top of his expensive jeans without taking his eyes off her face. "It . . . fits you very, um, very well."

Tristan lifted one shoulder carelessly. "It's expensive, but I find that you have to pay for quality."

Eve could see Lila struggling. "You should definitely buy it," she said, sounding a little breathless. "You will be supporting a local business, which is, um, very important."

Tristan reached over and plucked a flyer from Eve's fingers. "A little local festival," he said, glancing carelessly at the words. "How sweet. I'm sure my mum and the centre would *love* to participate."

Eve's fingers itched to slap his patronizing face. "Your mum isn't invited," she snapped. "The local businesses are going to do this by themselves, thank you very much."

Tristan looked bored. "Whatever," he sighed. "I'll take the shirt in this colour and the blue and grey," he told the shop owner. "Wrap the others for me, will you? I'll wear this one out." He plonked a credit card down on the counter

I can't let him get away with this, Eve thought passionately as the store owner rung up the transaction and handed Tristan the card and bag. "Your shopping centre isn't welcome here!" she shouted after Tristan's departing back.

He turned in the door, his striped carrier bag swinging between his fingers. Eve had a painful memory of a similar bag, hanging from the crook of her dad's elbow.

"You know what you are, Eve?" Tristan said. "A hypocrite."

Eve flinched as he winked at Lila and left the shop. He was right, and she hated him for it.

I used to be you, she thought in wonder. *I used to*

have what you have. Parties, clothes, influence. I used to think the shopping centre was the best idea in the world, because Daddy thought of it and Daddy never made mistakes. How could I have been such a fool?

"Eve," Lila began in a warning tone, but Eve had already left the shop, her whole body shaking with rage. She wouldn't let him get away with this. She would show him that the whole town was against him, him and his awful family and all their power and prestige. . .

She stopped on the pavement.

Shop owners were standing in their doorways, enjoying the sunshine and chatting animatedly with Ollie, Josh, Rhi and Polly. She could see flyers already posted on the lamp posts along the High Street, stuck on shop windows, clutched in shop owners' hands. The atmosphere had been energized, somehow, as if everyone had been plugged into a great switchboard of optimism. Laughter rang out down the street as she listened.

Selfish Eve is dead, she reminded herself. *I'm not doing this to spite Tristan de Vere. I'm doing this to help my town. My scruffy, quirky, funny little town.*

Building up is always better than knocking down.

This was going to make a real difference.

For the first time in a while, Eve felt truly proud of herself.

SEVEN

The Indian summer was still at full tilt as Eve walked along the High Street after school. Pulling her sunglasses from her school bag, she settled them on the end of her nose, and enjoyed the feeling of warmth through her school blazer. There wouldn't be many more days of this before autumn set in, and she planned to enjoy every drop of sunshine.

Glancing at the windows of the shops they'd targeted on Saturday, she frowned at the lack of flyers. She could have sworn there had been a hundred of them at the weekend, taped to lamp posts, doors, stuck under windscreen wipers and pinned to noticeboards. She spotted what looked like the ragged edge of a flyer fluttering a little pathetically on a lamp post halfway down the road. Someone had torn it down, leaving just one red corner remaining.

Eve sharpened her gaze, trying to find a flyer somewhere – anywhere. . . But all she could see were more red corners, and one or two torn and trodden scraps under her feet on the pavement.

She ducked into the men's clothes shop. "Excuse me," she said, trying to stop her voice from trembling with disappointment, "do you know what happened to all the flyers we put out at the weekend?"

The shop owner raised his hands. "A lad came along earlier and tore them all down," he said apologetically.

No need to ask for a description, Eve thought furiously. She did anyway.

"It was that dark-haired boy who was in here on Saturday buying one of my new-range shirts. You spoke to him, remember?"

Caitlin looked up from stirring her large coffee as Eve stormed into the little café on Marine Parade and threw herself down so hard into her chair that it creaked alarmingly.

"Blood pressure, darling," Caitlin said reprovingly,

pushing a large latte towards Eve. "A bright red face is not at *all* chic. Tell auntie Cait what's the matter."

"Tristan de Vere!" Eve burst out. "He's ripped down all our flyers!"

Caitlin didn't look as surprised as Eve had expected. "You have to expect a little opposition from the boy, Eve. His mother has very different plans for this town. You mustn't worry, because I have some truly marvellous news that will make Tristan de Vere spit."

Eve struggled to damp down the volcano of rage simmering in her breast. She took a deep breath, stirred her coffee and made herself drink the first sip as slowly as she could. Caitlin steepled her red-painted fingers and winked over the top at Eve.

"Every single business on the High Street has signed up to the festival," she said.

Eve almost spat out her coffee.

Caitlin sat back, pleased with the effect of her news. "And not only that," she went on with satisfaction, "I have had waves of interested sponsors contacting me all weekend. The Chandlers by the marina is going to offer boat rides out in the harbour on a specially decorated Christmas boat. This café is offering a gingerbread-making workshop, the art supplies shop is having a Christmas card competition. The funny little man who runs the hardware store behind the Heartbeat Café has a horse and trap, would you believe. He's planning to offer carriage rides along Marine Parade, complete with sleigh bells."

Eve could hardly take in so much good news at once. "You're joking!"

"I never joke about business." Caitlin took a dainty sip of her coffee. "And I haven't even told you about the weddings yet."

"Tell me now," Eve ordered.

Caitlin stirred her coffee before answering. "I should say wedding, singular, really," she mused, and for a moment Eve's heart sank before Caitlin's eyes glinted with mischief and she continued: "If you can call a mass wedding of forty people 'singular'."

Eve blinked. Had Caitlin said what she thought she'd said? "Forty people are all getting married at *once*?" she said in some disbelief.

"It's going to be huge," Caitlin said with satisfaction. "I think we should host it on the beach. We obviously need to sort out the permissions, but that won't be a problem. This town is Wedding Central, they must get crazy wedding requests all the time. Imagine all those wedding dresses, all those guests. Oh, and darling, the reception afterwards will be legendary. I'm planning on taking over the pier."

Eve's whole body thrilled as she imagined the buzz such an event would create. She felt a little dazed, picturing the great silver beach full of brides and grooms. "Bells," she said. "We'll ask all the churches in town for a mass bell peal for the wedding."

"What a lovely touch," Caitlin said, jotting it down. "It will really add to the atmosphere."

Through the whirl of her thoughts, Eve almost missed the buzz of her phone. She pulled it from her bag. Becca. She felt a little rush of guilt as she realized she hadn't thought about Becca all weekend. There had been too much planning to do, and her mind had been full of the Winter Wonderland and its possibilities. She ignored the call and slipped her phone away again. Becca would understand how important this was. She promised herself that she would call her back later.

Caitlin reached across the table and touched Eve's hand. "I've saved the best piece of news until last."

Eve felt winded all over again. "There's more?" she said, half laughing.

Caitlin stood up. "More coffee?" she asked breezily.

Eve begged and pleaded for her to sit down again, but Caitlin merely winked and headed up to the counter to order extra coffee and two large slices of carrot cake.

"Tell me!" Eve cried, laughing in exasperation as Caitlin made a big show of eating her carrot cake extra-slowly.

Caitlin set down her fork and patted the edge of her mouth with her napkin. "You know I mentioned national press?" she said at last, her eyes gleaming.

"Yes. . ."

"And magazines?"

"Get *on* with it, will you?"

Caitlin gave a great sigh. "Heartside Bay is possibly going to be featured in the Christmas edition of *Globa*."

Eve thought she'd misheard. The glossy travel magazine *Globa* lay on reception tables in all the most expensive hotels in the world. Its fashion spreads were legendary, its articles written by international journalists. "You don't mean—"

"If this goes well, Heartside Bay could be listed as one of their must-visit destinations this winter," Caitlin continued, as if she were telling Eve the most trivial piece of information in the world. "After Gstaad, of course, but above Salzburg. Oh," she added, "and if we're really good, we have a shot at being on the cover."

Heartside Bay on the cover of the Christmas edition of *Globa*? This was unbelievable. "Caitlin, how did you even speak to anyone at *Globa*, let alone get a scoop for Heartside like that?" Eve said, a little weakly.

Caitlin patted her fat notebook. "Contacts, darling. And of course, Heartside Bay *should* be world-famous. It's gorgeous. But we have to make sure it's good enough on the day."

Impulsively, Eve reached across the table and hugged Caitlin. "You're utterly brilliant," she said into her friend's expensively scented neck.

Caitlin patted Eve on the back and extricated herself. "There's just one teensy problem," she said. "They're sending a photographer and reporter down this Saturday, to take photos of Heartside."

"But that's good!" Eve exclaimed, struggling to understand Caitlin's point. "Isn't it?"

"They want to photograph Heartside Bay as it will look for the Winter Wonderland," Caitlin said. "Not as it looks right now."

Outside, the sun beamed through the café window. Eve shook her head like she had water in her ears. "They're coming this Saturday?" she repeated. "To photograph Heartside in winter?"

Caitlin lifted one elegant shoulder. "The press deadline for the Christmas edition is next week. I said it would be fine. You don't say no to *Globa*."

Eve felt the earth tipping beneath her feet. This was *Globa*. They had to make it work, the publicity would be worth its weight in gold. But how on *earth* were they going to make Heartside Bay in sunny September look like a Winter Wonderland in just five days?

EIGHT

Eve rubbed her eyes. Her lap was covered in tiny white flecks, her fingers were sore and her neck ached.

"You look like you're covered in snow, Eve," Lila giggled, lowering her scissors for a moment.

Eve brushed ineffectually at her skirt. The tiny slivers of sparkling white craft paper didn't budge. She'd lost count of how many snowflakes she'd cut out since they'd all arrived at Lila's place three hours earlier. Sixty? Seventy? *We need thousands*, she thought in some despair. "It's not me that needs to be covered in snow in five days," she said. "It's Heartside Bay. How many have you done now, Lila?"

"I lost count somewhere around eighty."

"Fifty-three," Josh announced, with some pride.

"I've done a hundred," Polly volunteered. She had sparkly shreds of paper in her hair. "Or thereabouts."

"How have you done so many, Pol?" Ollie demanded. His pile of failed snowflakes stood higher than his successes.

"All that sewing practice, I imagine," said Rhi, cross-legged on Lila's sofa where she was stringing snowflakes together on translucent wire.

"Stop yakking and cut," Eve ordered.

Everyone bent their heads obediently over their glittery tasks. *It's going to be worth it,* Eve told herself. She wiped her face with the back of her hand. *This is* Globa. *If everyone manages antoher fifty tonight, that'll be seven hundred and fifty. In three days, we'll have over two thousand.* Two thousand sounded like a lot. But would it be enough? Eve fretted over the question, cutting as quickly as she could.

Becca brushed a fleck of paper away from Eve's cheek. "You look like a snow princess," she said.

"Stop looking and keep cutting."

Becca sighed at her pile of uncut card. "I can't believe we're even attempting this. We must be crazy," she said. She waved her hands at the room, which looked as if a snowstorm had hit it. "Why are we spending all this time and money on a fake festival for one stupid magazine? Shouldn't we be focusing on the real Winter Wonderland instead?"

"Without the publicity *Globa* can bring us, there might not even *be* a Winter Wonderland," Caitlin reminded Becca. She trimmed more snowflakes and organized them in a pile beside Rhi.

Eve wished Becca would try to understand. "There are people's livelihoods at stake here, Becs," she said.

"My livelihood's at stake too," Becca replied a little sourly. "I told my boss I had to knock off at three every day this week. That's ten hours' work." She looked at her latest snowflake with some disgust. "And this doesn't even look like a snowflake. It looks like . . . I don't even *know* what it looks like."

"It'll be fine, Becca," Polly said soothingly as she took up another piece of card, her fingers flying as she cut out the distinctive snowflake shape.

Becca set down her scissors and stood up. She looked moodily down at her jeans, which were covered in icy-white glitter. "I need a break," she said, and left the room, shutting the door behind her with a bang.

Offering the others an apologetic glance, Eve got up and followed her girlfriend outside, trying to ignore the flash of pins-and-needles suddenly coursing through her legs.

"Are you OK, Becs?"

Becca gave a short laugh. "I feel like I'm covered in dandruff."

Eve took her girlfriend's hand. "I really appreciate you helping me," she said earnestly. "I know this isn't really your thing. But . . . it's really important to me, Becs. And to the town. Our Winter Wonderland is going to change things for Heartside Bay."

"Eve," said Becca with a snort, "we're cutting out paper. We're not saving the world. Seriously, why are we *doing* this? I don't get it. Selling things, I get. Ask the customers at my ice-cream parlour. Promoting things – sure, I can see the importance. But it seems to me that snowflakes are taking over our lives. In September. It's stupid."

Eve felt hurt. She was genuinely afraid that, even with two thousand snowflakes in the bag, they weren't going to pull this together in time for the *Globa* shoot at the weekend. Every time she pictured the professional photographer and journalist showing up, her blood ran cold. What if their efforts weren't enough? Eve could see all too clearly how pathetic anything but the best would look to a glamorous magazine like *Globa*.

I need you to understand how much fear I'm feeling right now, she thought. *I want you to hold me and tell me that everything's going to be fine. And I want you to share my excitement at this crazy adventure too. Because it* is *exciting*.

Instead, Becca was sulking.

Becca was different to her, Eve had always known that. More practical, more cynical, more grounded. It was part of the attraction, she supposed. But couldn't Becca even *try* to see how important this was for Eve?

"I've hardly seen you this week without a pair of scissors in your hands," Becca complained.

Eve suppressed the wave of tired irritation that was threatening to rise up and start an argument. "I'm sorry," she said pleadingly. "We will have some time together soon. Just us, I promise."

Becca muttered something under her breath. Eve took her hand.

"Please, Becs," she said. She felt so tired. "Let's not fight."

Becca's green eyes looked more gentle as she cupped Eve's face in her hands. "I'm sorry," she said. "I'm just tired of this. I miss you."

As they rested their heads together outside in the cool evening air, Eve felt a moment of peace.

"You mean so much to me, Becs," she said honestly. It was hard to convey in words just what Becca had done for her. "You've opened me up to so many new experiences. Helped me find myself."

"My pleasure," said Becca, a little gruffly. "I guess."

They kissed for a while. Eve found herself trying a little harder than normal to be loving, which made her feel nervous. The thing she loved about Becca was how she never had to pretend about anything. She sensed a gap opening between them. It was just a chink now, but Eve's stomach flip-flopped at the thought of it growing wider. Becca was her first girlfriend. How many people stayed with their first love for ever? *Not many*, whispered the voice in her head. She felt her gut clench. She didn't think she could bear it if she lost Becca. Not now, not after everything they'd been through together.

"I love you," she said a little desperately.

Becca didn't answer.

NINE

Eve brushed at her uniform as she hurried down the school corridor to collect her bag from her locker. She felt like she was permanently covered in glitter these days. She'd even dreamed about snowflakes the previous night. Every spare moment was taken up with cutting, making calls, organizing people. Her eyes felt gritty. She hadn't managed to wash her hair that morning, there simply hadn't been time. At least they were up to almost a thousand snowflakes now. With Rhi busy stringing them together on transparent filament wire, they were starting to look impressive. They just needed more of them.

She rounded the corner by the lockers. Tristan was lounging against the wall, his hands in his pockets, watching her approach with amusement in his black eyes.

"Snowing out there, is it?" he enquired.

"Drop dead," Eve replied as she lifted her chin and straightened her shoulders. There was no way she would let Tristan de Vere see how tired she was.

"How your little project going, anyway?"

Eve gritted her teeth as she opened her locker, pulling out her bag. "Really well, thank you for asking," she replied, swinging round to look him full in the face. "No thanks to you."

"I have no idea what you're talking about."

Eve pulled her bag close to her chest. It felt reassuring there, like she was wearing armour. "You know exactly what I'm talking about. We have more flyers, you know. Not to mention the whole of Heartside's retail community on our side."

Tristan cocked his head. "Not *all* of them," he pointed out.

"All the ones that count," Eve replied sweetly.

Tristan flicked a fragment of snowflake card off her shoulder. It drifted to the floor between them. "You're going to fail, you know," he said.

"Oh, I don't think so," Eve said, in as careless a voice as she could manage. "Everyone will be talking about Heartside Bay, come December. *Globa* are coming to shoot us on Saturday. We've got the front cover of the Christmas edition."

Tristan gave a sudden, swift smile that made her think of a crocodile spotting a meal on the riverbank. "I'm delighted for you," he said. "At least one thing in your life is working out."

Eve felt a flush stealing up her neck. For a moment, her composure deserted her. "If this is some low attempt at winding me up about my father—"

"Oh no," Tristan assured her, "everyone knows *he's* a disaster. It's your 'girlfriend' I'm talking about."

Eve could almost hear the quote marks he had put around the word. She'd never wanted to slap someone so badly in her life. "What about her?" she managed to say.

Tristan had already turned away. He stopped with a fake air of surprise, looking back at her. "You mean you don't know?" he said.

Eve felt a kick of dread. Was Becca OK? "What are you talking about?" she said, taking a step towards him.

Tristan pulled his phone out of his pocket with a lazy gesture, flicking through the photos. "I'm guessing this isn't you," he said, holding the phone under her nose.

Eve stared at the picture. It showed the beach shack where Becca had spent much of the summer selling ice creams. Two rickety tables sat on the sand in front of the shack, and at one of the tables were two girls holding hands. Eve gazed at Becca's chestnut hair. She switched her attention to the girl with the long black plait sitting opposite her girlfriend. Their hands were loosely linked across the table.

"You didn't know?" said Tristan. "Ah well." He slid his phone back into his pocket, raised his hand to his forehead in a kind of salute and sauntered away, whistling lightly.

Like that was even real, Eve thought with considerable scorn. Everyone had Photoshop these days. If Tristan thought he could upset her with a pathetic trick like that, he was even more stupid than he looked.

Her phone buzzed. A photo message and a text from Tristan.

L8rs. T

The photo would be fun to show to Becca, Eve decided, as her finger hovered thoughtfully over the delete button. They could laugh about it together. Right now, she could use a laugh.

She scrolled across the screen and pulled up Becca's number.

Meet after school? Xx

Becca responded at once.

Secret alcove. Will bring chocolate. xxx

Eve felt better at once. She slung her bag over her shoulder, brushed again at the perma-glitter on her shoulders, and headed out into the sunshine.

The wind was up today, and Eve enjoyed the way it raked through her hair as she walked down Marine Parade. A few more flyers were up, she was pleased to see. They would make this work if it killed her.

Tristan was just out to wind her up. *Given my plans*

to ruin the opening of his mum's shopping centre, fair enough, she thought. She even mustered the energy for a satisfied inner smile. He wouldn't succeed. When she set her mind to something, she usually got it.

Becca was perched on their usual rock. Eve hugged her warmly.

"What a day," she sighed, settling down beside Becca as her girlfriend handed her a bar of promised chocolate.

"You too?" Becca enquired. She sank her teeth into her chocolate, speaking with a full mouth. "We had a major disaster. Some kid with an allergy decided to help himself to a scoop of our walnut whip when no one was looking. His whole face blew up like a balloon."

Becca was good at embellishing stories, but this one sounded serious. "Was he all right?" Eve asked in some alarm.

"He was a nutcase," Becca said, with a wicked grin.

When Eve had finished laughing, she felt a hundred times better. She could usually rely on Becca to cheer her up.

"I've got a good one for you too," she said, pulling

out her phone. "Tristan de Vere tried to wind me up with this earlier." She passed Becca the photo at the beach shack. "It's quite good, actually – you can't see the joins. He's so *toxic*."

Becca studied the picture for a moment. "It's not Photoshopped," she said with a shrug, handing back the phone.

"What?" Eve said, a little stupidly.

Becca had the grace to look awkward. "She's called Clara. We met a few weeks ago at the shack."

Wait, Eve wanted to say. *This is a joke, right?* She realized she had her hands on her mouth. She lowered them. "You've been seeing a girl called Clara?" she repeated.

"We never said we were exclusive," Becca said awkwardly. "Besides, you haven't been around much lately. . ."

Eve felt like her entire ribcage had been removed from her body. She couldn't breathe. Quelling her panic, she forced herself to look Becca in the eye. "I thought. . ." She swallowed and tried again. "We never said that, no, but . . . Becca, you know how I feel about you."

"I know." Becca's expression was intent. "And I love you back, in a way. We have a history. You'll always be special. But this was never going to be serious, for either of us." She turned away.

Right now Eve was having trouble seeing anything beyond Becca's freckled face. The ghostly Clara with her long black plait seemed to shimmer on the rock beside them. She forced herself to laugh, as if none of this mattered, but it came out thin and reedy.

"This is your first relationship, Eve," Becca said in a gentle voice. "I don't underestimate its importance for you. But don't you think you should get out there and try on a few more people for size?"

I've never been dumped before, Eve thought. The gut-churning sensation was completely new to her.

She stood up. "You're a liar." She could feel her legs trembling. "It *was* serious. The way we felt about each other. . ."

"Maybe in the beginning," Becca admitted. "But lately. . . Eve, we weren't made to last. I love your spirit, your beauty, but I can't overcome our differences, you know?"

Eve felt tears spilling down her cheeks. She made no

effort to wipe them away. She simply stared at the girl breaking her heart into pieces.

"I'm sorry if you're hurt," Becca said honestly. "You're a lovely person. I know you'll find someone who'll understand you better than I do, who enjoys all the same things as you one day. Things like this festival, clothes, parties and all of that. Let's be honest, we both know I tolerate those things for you."

Becca was right, she supposed. Except for one thing. Eve knew with absolute certainty that she would never find someone to truly love and understand her, the way Becca said. She was too complicated.

The tears were cooling on Eve's face as the wind blew against her skin. "Life's too short to be with someone you tolerate," she said quietly. "If you really feel that way, then we need to end this."

As she spoke, Eve heard Madame Felicity's voice whispering on the afternoon wind. *I see many passionate relationships in your life,* the strange fortune teller had told her all those weeks ago. *But first you must forgive your father.*

"I'll always care about you," said Becca, trying to smile. "See you around, Eve. Look after yourself."

Eve watched Becca until she was out of sight. She couldn't imagine another relationship, ever, let alone a passionate one. And as for forgiving her father . . . *Like that's ever going to happen.*

She felt utterly alone.

TEN

It was more than an hour before Eve could muster the energy to leave the beach. Leaving her huddled perch on the beach rock made everything real. She felt like a scared traveller, leaving an island to strike out for new and unknown shores. Every part of her felt raw.

She had to think about something else, or she would go mad. *The Winter Wonderland*, she thought as she trudged up the sand, down the path and back towards the town. *Photo shoot, snowflakes, winter.* It suddenly wasn't difficult, she realized, to pretend it was winter. The sun was shining, but something cold had settled in her heart that made the world look and feel as bleak and dark as a December night.

She went home and sat in her window for a while.

The street view from the flat was very different to the view she'd had growing up: her large garden, her father's cars, the pool. Her mother and sister weren't home. They very rarely were these days.

Eve turned off her phone, took a long shower, and got into bed with a mountain of white card. She cut and cut and cut. The repetitive action was soothing. When she had cut a hundred snowflakes she lay down and turned off her light and stared unseeing at the ceiling until, at last, sleep descended.

"Don't hang it there," Eve said sharply, shading her eyes in the afternoon glow the following day. "The photographers aren't interested in the side streets. We need to focus on the High Street, how many times have I told you?"

Polly and Rhi exchanged glances, their arms full of glittering snowflake bunting.

"What?" Eve demanded, catching the look.

"Nothing," said Rhi after a moment.

"Are you sure you're OK?" Polly said, for what felt like the hundredth time today.

Eve hadn't told her friends about Becca. *I will*, she

thought. *But not yet*. Her heart was still feeling too tender. "Never better," she said firmly. "As long as you do what I say. We don't have time to do this all over again, we only have the rest of today and after school tomorrow and the photographer will be here. Josh!" she called. "Can you move the stepladder down the street? We need to get bunting up that lamp post!"

They had strung snowflakes along the most picturesque part of the High Street, where the road curved and narrowed and turned to cobbles as it swung towards the Old Town and the harbour. It was alarming how little bunting they had, despite all the hours of cutting. *Lucky we only have to decorate a hundred yards*, thought Eve, pushing her hair out of her eyes.

Her phone rang.

"The fake-snow suppliers don't have enough machines available for Saturday," said Caitlin's voice.

Eve took the blow as best she could. "Find another supplier. We only need snow along this stretch of the High Street, there must be more machines somewhere. Please, Caitlin, do what you can."

"The budget is getting smaller all the time, darling—"

"Promise them something," Eve said in desperation. "A free ride around the harbour during the festival, VIP tickets to one of your events, Cait, I don't know – *something*."

"Leave it to me."

Organizing events like this had been much easier in the old days, Eve reflected wearily as she tucked her phone into her back pocket. One call, one credit card number, and bang. It was amazing how she'd taken all that for granted.

She took a stroll down the short stretch of semi-decorated road, trying to take heart from the bustle and activity around her. Every shop window was filled with winter goods, cards and gifts. Eve had imposed a strict colour theme for the decorations – whites and dark forest greens only – and the result was gorgeous, calm and harmonious, the most elegant of Christmas cards.

She paused outside the stationers' shop, Paperweight. A pretty Christmas scene gazed out at her through the plate glass windows, but the whole thing was strangely dark.

"Polly, where are the twinkle lights for Paperweight?"

Polly looked apologetic. "There's something wrong with them, Eve, they won't turn on."

"There'll be a dodgy bulb," Ollie said, his arms full of white tinsel destined for the big white stage that had been erected beside the Ciao Café. "Someone will have to check them."

"There are five hundred bulbs in that string!" said Polly in horror.

"Just hope the dodgy bulb is near the beginning." It was the only comfort Eve could offer. There was too much else to do.

Her phone rang again. "Make it good news this time, Cait," she begged.

"We have another snow machine," Caitlin obliged. "However, you'll have to steel yourself a teensy bit, darling."

If I steel myself any more I'll turn into a robot, Eve thought. "What?"

"The mass wedding. We still have twenty interested couples, but the town hall has turned all particular, and the mayor is being very difficult about us using the beach. We may have to source a marquee instead."

Eve sank down on the pavement and rested her head on her knees, her ear still pressed to the phone. The mass wedding was the centrepiece of this whole photo shoot. She wondered whether Tristan's mother Annie de Vere had had a little "word" with the mayor. Her father had frequently used his own influence in town politics. Why wouldn't his replacement do the same?

"We don't have the money for a marquee," she said in despair.

"It's not looking good, darling, I agree."

What else can go wrong? she thought wearily as Caitlin hung up.

"Eve?" Lila was standing in front of her, wringing her hands. "You know the fund-raising Josh and I were doing to buy decorations for the central stage? We've fallen a bit short."

Eve wanted to cry. "How short?"

"About half a stage-worth," Lila said unhappily.

Eve rubbed the heels of her hands into her eyes. She hadn't felt this tired since her father's trial. "Then just

87

decorate half the stage," she said. Photography was all trickery, she reasoned. Maybe if they got the angle right. . . or was she just fooling herself?

"We have light!" Ollie shouted as Paperweight blazed into life. "The twenty-sixth bulb was the dud, how lucky is that?"

"He nearly started checking them from the other end," Polly giggled.

Eve still had no idea how they were going to fix the marquee problem, or the incomplete stage. But Polly and Ollie were both looking delighted with themselves, and the least she could do was congratulate them. "Good news," she said, forcing a smile. "Thanks."

"Hi, Dad," said Lila in sudden surprise as Chief Murray appeared around the corner of the Ciao Café, slotting his walkie-talkie back into his belt. "Where did you spring from?"

Chief Murray nodded absently at his daughter, but his eyes were on Eve. "Miss Somerstown," he said, "we need a word."

Step into my office, Eve wanted to say. She was feeling almost hysterical with tiredness. "Is there a problem?" she asked.

"I'm afraid there is." Heartside Bay's chief of police gave a heavy sigh. "I'm really sorry, but I'm going to have to shut you down."

Shop owners started coming out of their shops, staring curiously at Chief Murray and talking together in low voices. Halfway up the stepladder with his arms full of bunting, Josh looked down. Ollie and Polly put their heads out of the Paperweight doorway; Rhi and Brody laid down the cables and mics they were arranging on the main stage and craned their necks to try to catch the conversation.

"What are you talking about, Dad?" Lila gasped. "You can't shut us down, you can't!"

Chief Murray ignored her, steering Eve to the side of the street where they could talk in private. He took off his hat and turned it in his hands. "We've had a complaint," he said. "You haven't completed the appropriate paperwork to close off the High Street on Saturday for your photo shoot."

"I'll fill in whatever paperwork you need, right now," said Eve. She held out her hand. "If you can find a pen, I'll sign whatever you want, Chief Murray. I'm sure we can fix this." They *had* to fix this. *Globa* were coming.

"I'm afraid it's too late for that," the chief of police said. "Someone else has reserved the High Street for Saturday."

Eve didn't need to ask who. She was painfully aware that her father would have approached this problem in exactly the same way, once upon a time.

"Annie de Vere has several large cranes and trucks coming through town on Saturday," said the chief of police, confirming her worst fears. "She's bringing materials for the next phase of construction on the shopping centre. I'm sorry, but there's nothing I can do."

Eve wanted to scream. To stamp her feet and shake her fist at the stubbornly sunny sky and wail and cry. The marquee, the unfinished stage. . . and now this. It was a problem too far. After all her hard work, she was still going to fail.

ELEVEN

Eve climbed wearily down from the stepladder, her arms full of bunting. Part of her had wanted to run down the street, yelling and ripping the bunting apart. All that work. . . But that, of course, was precisely why she couldn't. Instead, she folded the bunting carefully over her arm and added it to the growing pile in the middle of the street.

"I'm so sorry," Lila groaned. "I feel like this is my fault, Eve."

"Your dad's just doing his job," Eve said. She was too sad even to shrug. She climbed back up the stepladder again, to fetch down more of the glittering snow decorations, while her friends watched her with worried eyes.

"I don't see why we can't leave it up there," Polly said, red-eyed from crying.

"Mrs de Vere's monster trucks will rip it to shreds when they drive down the High Street on Saturday," Ollie said gloomily, rubbing Polly's shoulder. "It's better we take it down. Stow it somewhere safe."

"We'll still use it for the festival," Rhi put in. "I'm sure Dad can store it for us in the Heartbeat Café."

"Have you cancelled *Globa* yet?" Josh asked.

Eve couldn't bring herself to make that particular call. "I'll do it later," she said. She couldn't believe they were going to miss out on such a golden opportunity, but life didn't always work out the way you wanted. She knew that better than most.

She took her phone out of her pocket and tried Caitlin again. Still no answer. Feeling even more bereft, Eve put her phone away again. She wanted someone to hold her. *Becca*, she thought a little tearfully. Becca would never hold her again. Not the way she wanted her to, anyway.

"Don't cry, Eve," said Lila. "Do you want me to call Becca?"

"No. Becca and I aren't together any more. She

ended it," Eve's voice cracked and she hated herself for it. "She's been seeing someone else. Ollie, help me move the stepladder, there's more bunting over there."

There was a further shocked silence from her friends. Eve was glad no one was offering condolences. In her present mood, she didn't think she'd be able to stand it.

As she climbed down the ladder with more bunting, Caitlin came rushing towards her, sunglasses clamped firmly on the end of her nose.

"What's up?" Eve said, jumping swiftly off the last few steps, her senses on high alert. "Why haven't you been answering my calls?"

"Too busy driving over here." Caitlin was uncharacteristically out of breath as she took Eve's hand. "Come on, we need to get to the police station."

The others started murmuring at each other in confusion. Eve didn't understand what was going on. "But—"

"Darling," Caitlin interrupted, "you really must learn not to argue with me. The others will start putting that bunting back up. Follow me, for heaven's sake."

She tugged Eve smartly along, her heels tapping fast and rhythmically on the pavement. Eve half-ran to keep up.

"Caitlin, please stop being so mysterious," she said. "Where are we going, and why?"

"We have a saviour," Caitlin said. "Mr Panayiotou, an olive-oil importer from Cyprus."

This made no sense. "Mr who?"

"I don't know either darling, but he's offered to put up the rest of the money we need for the mock Wonderland. He'll cover the costs of the marquee and the rest of the stage decorations. He's even offered to supply a couple of bands for the mass wedding reception."

Eve struggled to take in so much good news all at once. "Caitlin, how is this *possible*?"

"I have absolutely no idea," Caitlin said happily. "Isn't it marvellous? I love a mystery. Up the steps now."

Eve took the police station steps two at a time. "Cait," she tried to say, "even with all this money, we still have the problem with not having the right paperwork to close the High Street. Caitlin? *Cait!*"

The big double doors had swung shut in front of Eve as Caitlin disappeared inside the police station. Eve caught her breath for a moment, and pushed her hair back over her shoulders. Panayiotou. She'd never heard the name before. Why would an olive-oil importer fund her mock festival?

Drumming her long red fingernails on the reception desk, Caitlin was working her charms on the desk sergeant. "Be a darling and let Chief Murray know that Caitlin McManus and Eve Somerstown are here for him, would you?"

The desk sergeant looked a little dazed, but did as Caitlin instructed. Caitlin shot an excited grin at Eve as she sat down on a bench in the reception area and flung one leg over the other. She patted the bench beside her. "Sit down darling, you look fit to drop."

"I'm not sitting," said Eve clearly, "until you tell me how we're going to get out of this paperwork situation about the High Street. I take it Mr Panayiotou can't pull strings in the town hall?"

Caitlin opened the leather briefcase and rifled through the contents. Extracting a sheaf of documents, she waved them under Eve's nose. "A terribly helpful lawyer contacted me half an hour ago with something rather interesting about Mrs de Vere. Something that will fix everything. Trust me."

Eve frowned. Something here wasn't right. "Two complete strangers get in touch with you and make all our dreams come true just like that?" she said. "Don't you think that's rather strange?"

Caitlin wagged a finger at Eve. "I'm sure you've heard the expression, never look a gift horse in the mouth? It's very sound advice, darling. Horses have the *ugliest* teeth."

Chief Murray came out of his office, his eyebrows raised. "Yes?"

"Chief Murray," said Caitlin, sweeping through the door and sitting herself in front of the police chief's desk without waiting for an invitation. "The Heartside Bay Winter Wonderland Festival rehearsal must be permitted to go ahead this Saturday."

"As I explained to Miss Somerstown," Chief Murray began, "the High Street has been reserved by another party—"

"Mrs de Vere, yes," said Caitlin with a magnificent flick of her fingers. "But I think you'll find that she hasn't quite been following the rules." She pushed the sheaf of paper across the table towards the police chief. "A reliable source tells me that we're not the only ones who've got their paperwork wrong. According to town regulations, Mrs de Vere is not permitted to take vehicles over a certain weight down the High Street. I have worked out an alternative route for her juggernauts *here*..." She traced a road that led around the back of Heartside Bay – "and *here*, in order to get the required construction materials to the shopping centre. So now the High Street is available again, we are just *dying* to sign on that lovely little line and get our rehearsal up and running once more."

Eve gaped at Caitlin, smiling sweetly at the chief of police. Chief Murray studied the paperwork. Eve held her breath, dizzy with hope.

"Well," he said at last, smiling at them both over the top of the documents. "It would seem that you are correct, Ms McManus. If you will sign here and here, Miss Somerstown, I would be delighted to grant you permission to continue with Heartside Bay's Winter Wonderland rehearsal. I can only apologize for any inconvenience and wish you the best of luck in your enterprise."

Eve waited until they had reached the street before she flung her arms around her friend and squeezed her as hard as she could. "You're brilliant, Caitlin," she stammered. "Completely brilliant!"

"Don't thank me, darling," said Caitlin, setting her sunglasses on her nose again. "You must have a guardian angel keeping an eye out for you."

Eve felt as if she was on top of the world. *Globa* were still coming. The mock festival would be better than she'd ever envisaged, with all of the mysterious Mr Panayiotou's extra funding smoothing out the problems and paying for little details that would make all the difference. They could get as many snow machines as they wanted. The stage would look like an ice cave by the time she'd finished with it. This would be the best party she had ever had.

For a brief moment, thoughts of Becca intruded on her happiness. Eve put her ex-girlfriend gently to the back of her mind. She missed having Becca to share this wonderful news with her, but at least she had her friends.

We'll have a party tonight, she thought, *and I'll dress up as Father Christmas and give them all presents to thank them for all their hard work and for putting up with me.* She could only imagine how difficult she'd been to work with today. *Globa* would have the chicest front cover in the history of the magazine.

TWELVE

"Tristan alert," Rhi hissed.

Eve waved her salad fork at Rhi. Nothing could spoil her good mood today. "Let him come," she said. "If he wants to complain some more about the Winter Wonderland mock festival, we'll just remind him that paperwork is paperwork."

Lila giggled, smoothing her hair behind her ears as Tristan approached their table.

"Mind if I join you?" he said, his tray balanced in his slim brown hands.

"Yes," said Eve.

Ignoring Eve, Tristan settled down beside Lila, giving her a flirtatious look from under his eyelashes.

Josh glared, and crunched into his apple with considerable force.

"Eve said you weren't welcome, mate," said Ollie, half-rising from the table.

"Leave it, Ollie," Polly pleaded.

"I hear your little festival is trotting along like a well-behaved pony," Tristan said, taking a bite from his sandwich as Ollie muttered and sat in his place again.

"And *I* hear your mother's had to reroute her building materials," Eve countered.

"What my mum does with her bricks is none of my concern," Tristan shrugged. "But I *am* interested in the sort of friends you have, Eve."

Eve laid down her salad fork, steepled her fingers together and gave Tristan de Vere her steeliest look. If he wanted a fight, she'd give him one. "At least I *have* friends," she said, her voice full of mock sympathy. "I don't see anyone waving you over to their table."

"I'm not talking about friends in *here*. The kind you pass the time of day with and do whatever else passes for entertainment around this town," he said dismissively. "I'm talking about your *big* friends, out in the big bad world." He took another bite from his sandwich. "Or, to be more specific, *Daddy's* big friends."

Tristan grinned, catching the sudden tension in Eve's shoulders.

"Leave her alone, de Vere," Ollie growled.

"Oh, Ollie," Tristan sighed. "You are so out of your depth, you're drowning. I'm talking to *Eve*. It must be so nice having Daddy solving problems for you all the time, Eve."

"What are you talking about, Tristan?" Lila said.

Tristan's eyes never left Eve's. "It's just a shame that he has to fix your problems from behind bars."

Eve found herself on her feet, hating the smug-faced boy in front of her with every ounce of her being. Rhi and Lila had risen protectively on either side of her. People were starting to watch, sensing the rising tension from their table. She didn't want to be the focus of anyone's pity.

"Get away from me," she said in a low voice.

Tristan swallowed the last section of his sandwich and stood up. "Caitlin didn't tell you, did she? Daddy's still bailing you out, princess. Even from jail. Those two mysterious benefactors who got your shoddy little show back on the road? Daddy's pals."

People were talking now, pointing and whispering. Eve's friends faded into the background. It was just her and Tristan, and this battle they were fighting.

"You've outstayed your welcome," she said, gazing straight into his mocking black eyes. "Not that the welcome was there in the first place."

Smirking, Tristan left. Eve waited until he was out of sight before she too pushed back her chair. "I need some air," she said abruptly.

"Do you want me to come with you—" Lila began.

But Eve was already striding away from the canteen, her head hot and her thoughts whirling. Down the corridor, past the receptionist, down the white steps to the High Street. She stood for a moment in the road with her eyes closed, feeling the sun on her face and trying to work out how she felt.

Her first thought was of gratitude, she realized with surprise. Her dad was still there, watching out for her, and it was a good feeling. She had no idea how he had pulled the strings from jail, but if Tristan was right – and she knew he was right – he had. In a funny way, she admired her father for it. *Best dad in the world*, she thought wryly.

But her pride was dented too. Her dad still thought she couldn't handle things by herself. He hadn't thought to tell her what he was doing, he hadn't trusted her. He still thought of her as a child in need of help. And by keeping his secrets, he had left her open to Tristan's taunts.

I've grown up since you went away, Dad, she thought. *More than you can imagine.*

But there was no denying that her dad had always supported her. He had been wrong about so many things but she was still lucky to have him. Perhaps it was time to tell him that.

Eve walked down the High Street, shrugging off her blazer in the heat and tying it around her waist. School could wait. She would catch the bus and see her father. She had to thank him for saving the Winter Wonderland, at least.

As the bus rumbled through the town and out towards the prison, Eve felt lighter. Making the decision to visit her father had lifted a weight from her shoulders. She was almost looking forward to the visit.

The feeling didn't last. It occurred to her as she half-ran, half-walked down the street towards the jail from the bus stop that she didn't have a visiting order. Jails stuck by the rules. How would she get in to see him? She paused in dismay, worrying about the practicalities of what she was trying to do. All the charm in the world wouldn't get her past the guards, she knew that much. Prisons were prisons for a reason.

I'll leave a message, she thought. *They'll let me do that, won't they?*

She joined the trickling crowd shuffling through security. Several yards ahead of her, she saw a familiar-looking profile.

"Mr Munroe?" she blurted in surprise.

Her father's lawyer turned to stare at her. "Eve?" he said. "What are you doing here? Aren't you supposed to be in school?"

This was too good an opportunity to pass up. Eve shouldered past the other people in the line, ignoring their muttered oaths and dirty looks. "Mr Munroe! Are you here to see Daddy? I need to see him too, please help me, I don't have a visiting order but—"

"Keep some order in the line please—"

Eve was desperate to make Mr Munroe understand. She gripped his suited arm, trying to ignore the jostling around her. "Please, he's helped me and I need to talk to him, he thinks I hate him but I *don't*."

"No need for a visiting order, Eve," said Mr Munroe. "You can tell him yourself tomorrow. He's being released."

THIRTEEN

"I don't understand," said Eve after a shocked pause. She wanted to badly to believe Mr Munroe, but. . . *That's not right,* she wanted to say. *Daddy was sentenced to jail for nine months, not three.*

"Move along, please," said the bored security guard.

Eve brought her scattered thoughts back together. "Mr Munroe, perhaps you can explain this to me once we're through security. I want to come in with you and see him. Can you arrange that?"

Mr Munroe looked doubtful. "I'm here on official business."

"Don't lawyers sometimes have assistants?"

"Yes, but I don't think. . ." As if recollecting where

he was, Mr Munroe lowered his voice. "I don't think lying in this situation is a good idea."

Eve looked him squarely in the eye. "You've lied for Daddy before."

Mr Munroe gaped. With his reddish hair and bulging eyes, he reminded Eve of a goldfish. "What did you say?"

Doing it this way was below the belt, Eve knew, but desperate times called for desperate measures. "Mr Munroe," she said in her most confidential voice, "I don't want to get you into trouble, but I saw Daddy's laptop. The one you handed over to the authorities at the trial."

"I. . . There was no impropriety on that laptop, Miss Somerstown, I'm shocked that—"

"Maybe there wasn't when you handed it in," Eve said, turning the screw, "but there was when I saw it. A few bank accounts that shouldn't have been there. With your name on them."

"Next," called the security guard.

"If you take me in with you, this need go no further," Eve continued. The lawyer's eyes were darting around frantically. She knew she was right about this.

"What's past is past, Mr Munroe." She smiled at him. "I just want to see my father."

Five minutes later, she had deposited her personal belongings and was following the red-faced lawyer triumphantly down the bleach-smelling corridor.

Her euphoria faded the moment they set foot in the visiting room.

"Daddy!" she croaked, frozen to the spot as she stared in horror at the man in front of her.

Her father's face was a rainbow of colours from green to yellow to purple. One eyelid was almost swollen shut. "Well, *you're* a sight for sore eyes," he joked through thick, bruised lips. "Munroe, I should give you a payrise for this. Evie, what a surprise for an old man! I can't tell you how pleased I am to see you."

"What happened?"

"Nothing to worry about."

Eve felt a wave of anger, towards her father and whoever had done this to him. "Daddy, I'm not a child any more. Stop protecting me! I asked you a question, and I think I deserve an answer. *What happened?*"

Her father patted the air. "Sit down, honey. It was a fight, nothing more. There's a lot of fighting in here.

Munroe, how is it that you've brought my daughter today?"

"We met outside," Munroe said stiffly. He had opened a briefcase and pulled out a clear plastic wallet of documents.

"Did Munroe tell you, princess?" said her father, trying to smile at her with his bruised lips. "I'm getting out of here tomorrow morning at nine o'clock. Isn't that great?"

"Why are they letting you out early?"

"Let's not go into such boring details," said her father dismissively. "The important thing is that I'm coming out. I'll be back at home with you and your sister, Evie. And your mother too, if she'll still have me."

Privately, Eve doubted that. Her mother had been spending a suspicious amount of time in London recently. The last time her mother had come back to the flat, she'd been getting out of a large Range Rover driven by a man with silver hair and a very expensive watch.

"I have some paperwork, Henry," said Munroe. "If you could sign these for me?"

Eve watched as her father scribbled his flamboyant signature across the forms Mr Munroe was handing him. Her mind was full of questions, but also doubts. She wanted to forgive her father. He looked so vulnerable in his bruised and bearded state, but he was still keeping secrets from her. He was getting out early for reasons he wasn't prepared to share, that much was clear. She knew him well enough to work that out for herself.

"We'll discuss the rest tomorrow, Munroe," her father said in shades of his old business tone, passing back the last handful of documents to his lawyer. "So Evie, your old dad will be back in your life from tomorrow morning. What do you think about that?"

Eve remembered why she had come. Her father's latest secret would have to wait. "Daddy," she said, "I wanted to thank you for helping me to save the Heartside Bay Winter Wonderland rehearsal. I really appreciate it."

"You worked that out, did you? I'm still watching out for you, princess."

He tapped his nose indulgently at her. Eve was reminded of a birthday party she'd once had, when he had booked her favourite band without telling her – at what had probably been vast expense. *I've missed you so much*, Eve thought. *But I deserve more than this.*

"Don't do it again," she said steadily. "Not without telling me first."

Her father's face took on a sheepish expression. "Baby, you had it all under control, I know, right up until the last moment. I still have ears in the community, friends who haven't disowned me completely. They told me what a great job you had been doing for local businesses. I couldn't sit back and let all that hard work go to waste because of Annie de Vere."

"Don't do it again without talking to me first," Eve repeated. "You owe me more trust than that."

Her father stared at her. "You have grown up, haven't you princess? I promise I'll ask you in future, OK?" He held up his fingers in the "Scout's Honour" position, and laughed. "I promise you that when I get out this will all seem like a bad dream. I have plans to get our family back to the top of the tree. Don't look at me like that, sweetheart, it's all legitimate this time. I'll pull us all back, and it will be better than it ever was, because we'll have honesty this time. And you'll be right beside me. My best princess."

He took her hand and squeezed it and smiled at her. And Eve badly wanted to believe him. *Maybe I will get my life back the way it once was*, she thought. She glanced around the visiting room, at the bars discreetly set into the windows, at her father's prison uniform and his swollen black eye. *And maybe pigs will fly.*

She shook her head, and gently removed her hand from his fingers. "I love you Daddy," she said honestly, "but I still don't believe you. I don't trust you, you see. I wish I did, but I don't."

Her father paled. He stroked his bruised eye, struggling for something to say. "You love me, do you?" he said eventually. "Well, that's a start, I suppose."

"Promise me you'll never put our family through this again," Eve demanded.

"I . . . will try my best, sweetheart."

In a way, she found the hesitancy in his answer encouraging. It meant, at least, that he was thinking a little harder before building castles in the air. She hoped the trust would come back, eventually. One day. Maybe.

FOURTEEN

The sun beat down relentlessly on the wintery scene. The shop windows were perfect, wreathed in whites and greens, their twinkle lights glowing, their displays tempting Christmas pockets. The snowflake bunting hung in shining lines overhead, dangling over the cobbled end of the High Street and catching the sun as the snowflakes spun and twirled in the breeze. The stage was wreathed in so much white tinsel it looked like a half-exploded iceberg. It was the hottest day of September, and the mock Winter Wonderland had begun.

"More snow!" Eve shouted to Josh and Ollie.

Josh pushed his hat back from his sweating

forehead. "We're doing the best we can," he protested. "But everything's melting as soon as it touches the warm ground. Can you turn up the air-conditioning units?"

"On it," said Polly, hurrying over to the large air-con units stationed discreetly at the corner of the road. There was a whirr and a roar, and the hot air grew fractionally cooler.

"This is lovely," Lila sighed, standing with her arms beside the nearest unit, letting cold air blow through the woollen jumper and jeans she had agreed to wear for the photo shoot. "I could stand here all day."

"That air's not meant for you, Lila." Polly pointed at the magnificent ice sculpture of a prancing reindeer a little further down the street, whose antlers looked suspiciously shiny. "It's meant for Rudolph."

"Just a couple more minutes," Lila begged. "I'm melting just as much as Rudolph is!"

Eve knew how Lila felt. "No time," she said briskly. She adjusted the woolly beanie on her own head, feeling the sweat trickling down the back of her neck. "Caitlin, any progress on the *Globa* reporters?"

"They're parking, darling. Should be with us in five.

Rhi, can you sing us something festive to keep us in the mood?"

On the stage, Rhi adjusted her microphone, fiddled with the fluffy earmuffs she had clamped over her ears and started singing "Winter Wonderland". She sang to the jolly backing track pumping out of the sound system that hung on either side of the stage.

Josh sang back to her, wrapping his scarf a little more loosely around his neck.

The watching shopkeepers laughed and fanned themselves in the heat as Polly handed out woolly mittens and extra scarves.

Rhi sang on, pulling a face at Josh. Brody joined her for the chorus, leaning in to the microphone beside her.

Beyond the stage, the icy-white turrets of the great wedding marquee rose above the shop roofs, covering the car park beside Marine Parade, like an enormous snow castle with its fluttering pennants of green and gold. It *did* look like a Winter Wonderland, Eve thought in satisfaction. It looked incredible.

Caitlin linked arms with Eve as Josh sprayed a great arc of snow across the middle of the street. "We've worked miracles here, darling," she said. "This is all *beyond* chic."

Eve mopped her forehead. She hated to think what the beanie was doing to her sweat-soaked hair. Checking her watch, she dug her hand into the bag she was carrying. "Time for the jumper," she said with a grimace. "Wish me luck."

She had just pulled the prickly woollen jumper over her head when she saw the photographer and reporter walking swiftly towards her. Adjusting her hat as quickly as she could and doing her best to ignore the awful scratchy sensation of the wool over her vest top, she plastered a smile on her face. "Welcome to Heartside Bay," she began. "It's a real honour to have *Globa* magazine shooting us today, we hope you like what we've done to showcase Heartside's many—"

The reporter thrust her microphone under Eve's nose. "Miss Somerstown, can we get your first impressions on the news that your father has been released from prison today?"

Eve's smile froze to her face. "This is a photo shoot for the Heartside Bay Winter Wonderland, I don't think my personal business is relevant—"

A photography bulb had flashed in her face. The

reporter pressed on excitedly. "Can you forgive your father for putting you and your family through so much misery? How is he going to make amends? Why has he been released early?"

Pop. Another flashbulb. Eve put her hand up to shield her face.

"That's enough," said Caitlin sharply, moving in front of Eve as the camera flashed for a third time. "This is not the time for your questions."

"Yeah, push off," added Ollie. The bobble on the top of his hat added several useful inches, and the reporter looked wary as he advanced towards her. "Can't you see we're busy?"

I have to speak to them, thought Eve, recovering herself as best she could. "It's OK, Ollie," she said, and faced the reporter. "I believe that everyone deserves forgiveness and second chances. Now, would you excuse us? We're very busy today."

"Miss Somerstown—"

"She's given you a quote," Ollie interrupted. "Pol? Let's show these two back to their car."

Polly joined her boyfriend in ushering the reporter and photographer away from the scene. She glanced back over her shoulder to give Eve an encouraging smile. Eve smiled weakly back. The timing of her father's release couldn't have been worse. She hoped it wouldn't ruin everything she'd worked for. She wanted to world to be talking about Christmas in Heartside Bay, not Henry Somerstown, their disgraced ex-mayor.

Caitlin stiffened beside Eve. "Here they come, darling."

The reporter and photographer from *Globa* had just turned into the High Street, and were studying the Christmas decorations, talking quietly together. It was clearly them, to judge from their city clothes and equipment. The photographer was already firing his shutter. Eve recovered. It was show time.

She waved at Rhi and Brody. "Winter Wonderland" started up again as Josh obligingly sprayed the air with snow. Turning her face up to the whirling whiteness, Eve allowed herself a smile as she gathered her thoughts in preparation for *Globa*'s questions. It may not really have been Christmas, but it was close.

She felt Lila tap her shoulder. "We have a problem, Eve."

Eve opened her eyes and stared at the figure walking

towards them through the whirling snowflakes, his hands in his pockets, his bruises yellowing, the familiarity of his silhouette bringing an ache to her throat. "It's OK," she said, her eyes fixed on her father. "I'm ready."

"Not that problem," Lila said unhappily. "A different problem."

Annie de Vere looked like her son, the same full dark hair, the same piercing eyes. Suddenly transfixed, Eve watched her approach from the opposite direction with Tristan on her tail. The reporter and photographer that Polly and Ollie had been trying to get rid of reappeared, scenting a fresh story, camera and notepad poised. Her father didn't break his step. At this rate he and his business rival would crash into each other. The *Globa* team hadn't noticed – yet.

Eve was reminded suddenly of a scene from the Wild West, outlaw and sheriff, spurs jingling, eyes watching through shuttered windows as they strode into battle. If she didn't do something fast, tomorrow's headlines would have nothing to do with Heartside's Winter Wonderland at all – and all their hard work really would have been for nothing.

FIFTEEN

For a moment, time rolled away from Eve. Her dad was coming towards her, smiling, wearing a familiar suit, which hung loosely from his slighter frame. His shoes gleamed with polish, his face was clean-shaven. It was as if the past few months hadn't happened. For an instant, she was ten years old again, and her father was fresh back from a business trip abroad with his arms full of gifts. And it didn't matter that the sun was blazing down on her woolly hat, or that her feet were slipping in unseasonable snow, or that her jumper itched. She just wanted to feel her father's arms around her.

"Daddy!" she half-choked, and broke into a run.

"Eve, wait!" Lila called, giving chase.

Lila's voice shocked some sense of reality back into Eve. She slowed her pace, almost skidding on a blob of half-melted snow on the road. The moment she reached her father, they embraced – but Eve pulled back at the last moment, wary and confused, and the kiss she felt on her cheek was fleeting.

"Evie." Her father's smile was hopeful but strained. "I love the outfit."

Eve pulled herself together. "Daddy, Mrs de Vere is here and we have a photo shoot. There are reporters from the press but I have to focus on the reporter from the travel magazine and the snow is melting and—"

Her father understood. "I can handle de Vere, princess. Leave it to me. Lila, isn't it?"

Hovering on the pavement a few paces behind Eve, Lila nodded shyly.

"Distract de Vere's son for me, will you?"

Giving Eve a swift nod, Henry Somerstown shepherded Lila back down the road towards the great white stage. Eve saw her father briskly shaking Annie de Vere's hand with both of his. Her father could turn on the charm like a tap when he wanted to. It was a useful skill, Eve realized.

Tristan flicked his eyes warily towards Eve, but Lila had leaned up to him and was whispering something in his ear. You could say what you liked about Lila Murray, but when it came to distracting boys, there was no denying her expertise. In the stress of the moment and under the watchful eyes of the press reporter, Eve wanted to giggle. *Don't wade in with your fists flying, Josh,* she thought, checking the street for Lila's vigilant boyfriend. *Not this time.*

"So Annie, I have a couple of business propositions that I'm sure will interest you. . ." Henry Somerstown was leading Annie de Vere to one side, keeping his back to the press photographer, his free hand gesturing eloquently in the air. Tristan followed meekly as Lila tugged him along with her. Eve watched her father place a paternal hand on Tristan's shoulder, drawing him into the conversation, then throw a ghost of a wink in Eve's direction. His meaning was as clear as glass. *I thought you had a job to do. Get on and do it!*

Eve adjusted her beanie one last time and hurried back to Caitlin. The *Globa* photographer and reporter had finished their preliminary notes and photographs,

123

and were bearing down on Eve with professional smiles in place.

Eve suddenly remembered the little gift baskets she and Caitlin had assembled the previous evening. They had arranged all the treasures they had begged from local businesses – sample bottles of shampoo and mini boxes of chocolate, a pair of cashmere socks donated by the men's clothing shop, a pack of hand-printed Christmas cards from the stationers – in baskets filled with snow-sprayed leaves, their wooden handles decorated with festive holly berries and finished with a handwritten labels: *with Christmas love from the Love Capital of England.*

"The baskets!" Eve hissed at Caitlin in horror. "We haven't—"

"Darling," Caitlin interrupted reproachfully, "you didn't think I'd forget something so very important?" She pulled her hands from behind her back, dangling the little baskets from two gloved fingers.

"Eve Somerstown? Roger Deauville, from *Globa* magazine. This is Lorenzo Mazzoli, my photographer. You *have* been busy, haven't you?"

Eve swung back to the reporter with her widest

smile. "Roger," she said in her most practised hostess voice. "What a long way you've come, I can't tell you how much we appreciate it." She pressed the baskets into the men's hands. "I do hope you enjoy these little gifts. It's just a little taste of everything Heartside Bay has to offer the Christmas shopper."

"Charming," said Roger, stroking the cashmere socks with approving fingers. Setting the basket down, he shook Eve's hand firmly, then pushed back his Panama hat and studied the scene with amusement. "The hottest Christmas on record, I think we can safely say. Lorenzo? Blue filters, I think."

"You do your job, *Ruggiero*, and I will do mine," said the photographer in a thick Italian accent. He winked at Eve as he slid a deep blue filter over the lens of his extraordinarily expensive-looking camera and fired a succession of shots at the white stage.

Eve and Caitlin took the two men on a tour, introducing them to the shop owners, encouraging them to sample the mulled wine at the delicatessen. Caitlin flirted with Lorenzo the photographer, draping him in the fine knitted scarves on display in the men's clothes shop and feeding him roasted chestnuts, while

Eve fired her carefully practised soundbites at Roger Deauville, and almost forgot to feel hot in her winter clothes.

"Heartside Bay specializes in supporting local craftsmanship. We're spoiled for choice in this area. Pottery, textiles, jewellery, even wine – we have our own microclimate on the south coast, which can rival the Mediterranean."

Roger Deauville squinted in the bright sun. "It's certainly rivalling the Med today," he joked.

With his hat tipped back on his head in a style that reminded Eve of Josh, the journalist listened intently, sampling food, holding delicate hand-blown glass goblets up to the light, firing instructions at Lorenzo to photograph a perfectly arranged stack of rainbow-hued blankets on a heavy oak shelf, a hand-carved Nativity scene in the prettily lit window of a gift shop, the large Christmas tree imaginatively hung with striped silk slippers in the shoe shop. Eve wanted to skip for joy at every nod of approval. Would *Globa* be able to resist Heartside Bay's imagined winter charms? Were they really going to get the front cover of Europe's most coveted travel magazine?

Her phone buzzed.

Brides and grooms ready when you are. Ollie
xx

"Of course," said Eve smoothly, putting the lightest pressure on Roger Deauville's linen sleeve as she guided him away from the last shop on their tour and down the uneven, snow-scattered cobbles towards the harbour, "Heartside Bay isn't just beautiful on the outside, but on the inside too. Welcome to the centrepiece of our Winter Wonderland."

The great white marquee's snowy canvas sides were swathed heavily with white roses and glossy holly and ivy leaves, white voile curtains blowing in the salty summer breeze. Lorenzo exclaimed under his breath and fired a dozen shots at the heavy curtain of white roses framing the main entrance.

Inside, the sense of Christmas fantasy continued. Great green Christmas trees studded with white lights stood in the place of supporting marquee pillars, giving the impression that Eve, Caitlin, Roger and Lorenzo were walking through a twinkling evergreen forest.

Eve glimpsed Ollie and Polly peering around the piney-scented trunks like woodland sprites in matching green bobble hats, offering her smiles and thumbs-up before ducking away again.

Twenty couples stood before a vast green tree at the heart of the marquee, hands clasped, heads turned towards the white-and-gold platform where the registrar, beaming in a long white cassock, began to speak.

"We are gathered here on this joyful occasion to witness the joining in matrimony of no fewer than forty persons here present."

From the middle of the mass wedding, Polly's mum and her partner Beth Andrews turned and winked at Eve. Ollie's parents were there, reaffirming their vows, and other familiar faces dotted the ice-white floor. Black, white, straight, gay, old and young – the great mock wedding had it all.

"*Mamma mia,*" said Lorenzo, forgetting to lift his camera and staring at the sheer number of people all pretending to get married at once in this magical Christmas glade.

The reporter and photographer stood quietly at the

edge of the ceremony as the vows rolled out together among the scented trees. "To have and to hold, from this day forward, for better, for worse, for richer, for poorer, in sickness and in health, until death do us part. . ."

Forty pairs of lips came together to exchange tender kisses. The marquee erupted in applause, cameras flashing.

"What an extraordinary experience," said Roger Deauville as they filed back outside into the heat of the summer sunshine. "I thought I'd seen it all, but that was something else."

"*Bellissima*," sighed Lorenzo Mazzoli.

For the first time that day, Eve felt tears catch at the back of her throat. *Oh, Becca*, she thought sadly. She couldn't imagine even falling in love again.

SIXTEEN

Eve and Caitlin showed Roger Deauville and Lorenzo Mazzoli around the beautiful boat they had booked to take people out on Christmas cruises around the bay during the festival. It was looking its best for the photo shoot, its shining wooden masts strung with white lights, ribbons and Christmas bells that tinkled as the boat dipped and rose in the swell of the harbour.

"I think they like it," Eve whispered as Roger Deauville got into an animated conversation with the captain. "Oh, but Cait – do you think they like it enough?" Even though the day had gone well so far, there was still a part of her that couldn't believe they would ever get the *Globa* Christmas front cover.

Surpremely unconcerned, Caitlin was applying powder to the tip of her nose. "Of course they like it, darling. When will you learn that we are extremely good at what we do?"

"Are we taking her out?" Roger asked, stroking the wooden mast and casting a hopeful look at the glittering bay.

"*Ruggiero*, we have no time," said Lorenzo, tutting as he fired his camera at the deck, then back at the scenic view of Heartside Bay clustered around its great silver beach in the waning afternoon sun. "We have to file this copy tonight or we will not make our print deadline."

In the brief half-hour they had spent in the harbour, the marquee had been transformed for the mass wedding reception. With the air finally darkening outside, the illusion of a Christmas evening felt more solid than ever. Tables stood where the couples had exchanged their vows. A great glitter ball turned above the snowy white tablecloths with their green and cream place settings, and the dais where the wedding registrar had spoken the words of the marriage ceremony was stacked with amps, microphones and assorted instruments. The band for the evening was to be fronted by Rhi and Brody, who waved as Eve and Caitlin ducked among the twinkling pine branches with their guests.

Roger Deauville moved among the guests, asking questions and making notes, while Lorenzo changed filters and lenses and took a hundred more photographs. Eve tried her hardest not to bite her nails as she waited for *Globa*'s final verdict on all their hard work.

"I don't know why you're looking so worried, Eve," said Josh, sitting with the others at a large table set a little way back from the stage. "Your reporters would be mad not to promote the Heartside Bay Winter Wonderland."

"Have you seen how many memory sticks Lorenzo has been through?" Lila put in. "I saw him change at least five, and that was before you guys even set foot on the Christmas cruise boat."

"If they weren't interested they would have left by now," Polly added, which Eve supposed was true.

"Psst," Ollie hissed.

Eve smiled, feeling slightly terrified as Roger Deauville and Lorenzo Mazzoli appeared at their table.

"Eve," said Roger, shaking her hand warmly. "It's time for us to go. Lorenzo has taken some terrific shots, and I have more copy than I know what to do with. I'm delighted to confirm that Heartside Bay will be on the front cover of our Christmas edition."

Eve let out a breath she hadn't even known she was holding as her friends started cheering and clapping around her.

"There's nothing like it in the UK," Roger went on, smiling through the noise. "If the real deal is anything like the dress rehearsal, I feel sure it will be an enormous success for you all. I plan to send a few of the photos to the national press as well, so that they know about it and run plenty of publicity for you. Thank you for a wonderful day. I can only imagine how much hard work it took to bring winter to Heartside Bay today, but you pulled it off."

Eve shook Roger's hand in a daze, and exchanged kisses with Lorenzo, and as the reporter and photographer left amid a flurry of waving and hand-shaking, she sank down on her chair and buried her face in her hands.

The word travelled around the marquee in a flash.

Heartside Bay's festival would make the front cover of the world's most prestigious travel magazine. A bumper Christmas for all the small businesses who had taken part in the day's vast mock event was guaranteed. The whole place seemed to erupt in cheers and applause. Every eye in the marquee was turned towards Eve and her table.

"You did it!" Lila screamed.

"*We* did it," Josh corrected.

"Can I take off my bobble hat now?" Ollie asked.

Rhi and Brody both leaped off the stage with a whoop and rushed towards them to join the celebrations. Eve held out her arms to her friends, and everyone bundled together in an ungainly woolly-jumpered hug, kissing and crying and laughing. She couldn't begin to express how grateful she was to them all, for everything they'd done for her today.

I think we just made a difference, she thought in a daze. Today had been better than Christmas.

"We all deserve a party," she said, when she could speak. "Rhi, Brody, what are you doing down here? You have an audience! Go sing Christmas songs!"

Rhi and Brody headed back to the stage, where

the band struck up a lively rendition of "Frosty the Snowman". People had started dancing, couples from earlier swaying together with their heads on each other's shoulders. Lila dragged a protesting Josh on to the dance floor; Ollie did the same with Polly. People were drifting among the Christmas trees, marvelling at the decorations, feasting on these strange rumours of Heartside Bay's impending fame, curious and happy and ready to celebrate.

"Well done," said Caitlin, patting Eve's hand.

"Thanks, Caitlin." Eve's face hurt from so much smiling. "I couldn't have done it without you."

"That goes without saying, darling."

Through the crowd, Eve glimpsed her father's silvery head. She stood up as he approached her table.

"Evie," said her father warmly, taking her hands. "*Globa* front cover, I hear. You've pulled this town together, made the impossible happen. I'm so proud of you." He made a rueful face. "I just hope I can make you proud of me again, some day."

His words of praise washed through Eve like balm, filling a gap she hadn't even known was there. *I hope so too*, she thought, holding tightly to her father's hand, but her heart was too full to speak the words aloud.

Rhi sang old Christmas songs softly into the microphone as the dance floor swayed together.

Henry Somerstown held out his hand to his daughter. "Dance with me?"

Eve let her father put his arms around her, drawing her to the dance floor, to sway with her to the evergreen words of the old song. At last, she felt safe, protected, and loved.

Over her father's shoulder, Eve saw a familiar figure enter the tent, his arm around the waist of the most beautiful girl she had ever seen. Her mood dipped in dismay. Tristan de Vere was here – and he had a date.

You're not spoiling this, she thought fiercely as Tristan shepherded the girl towards her with a mocking smile on his face. *I won't let you.*

SEVENTEEN

Her father felt her stiffen against him. He pulled back and frowned down at her. "What's up, princess?"

"Tristan de Vere," Eve replied through gritted teeth.

But she wasn't able to say any more, because Tristan was in front of her, smiling that infuriating smile of his.

"I'll leave you youngsters to chat," said her father, kissing Eve on the cheek.

Eve wanted to call him back, but he'd already disappeared in the crowd, one hand lifted in farewell. Now it was just her and Tristan and the girl – who, Eve noted, was even more beautiful close up.

"What are you doing here, Tristan?" she said, trying not to let the girl's perfect heart-shaped face distract her.

"It's a party. Parties need guests, last time I looked."
Tristan looked incredulously around at the dancefloor,
the odd assortment of everyday clothes, old wedding
dresses, dusty, danced-on shoes, hastily arranged hair
and make-up running in the evening heat. "Where did
you *find* all these creatures? Rent-a-Bride?"

She could tell Tristan wanted her to make a
scene. To shout at him, throw him out. To make
this evening all about him. She understood it all in a
flash: the bored and beautiful boy, keen to win back
the spotlight that he had so inexplicably lost. *It's not
going to work,* she thought. *I won't give you that
satisfaction.*

"If it's all so beneath you," she said sweetly, "why
are you here?"

"I wanted to show Gabriella what passes for a good
time in this sad little town," said Tristan with a sniff.
He waved his hand at the girl beside him. "Gaby, this is
Heartside Bay's hostess with the leastest, Eve. Eve, this
is my cousin Gabriella."

I won't let you beat me, Eve thought. She glared at
Tristan, her chin held high. Then she switched her icy
attention to Gabriella, fully prepared to fight her as well.

"Hi," said Gabriella. And she smiled.

Eve felt her mouth go dry. How was it possible for anyone to be so beautiful?

"Aren't you going to kick me out?" Tristan enquired. He grinned. "I love a good scene."

Gabriella's eyes were the most perfect shade of blue-grey and her lashes were long and thick. She had high cheekbones, perfect skin, long dark hair. The way she was looking at Eve was making her feel weak.

"Enjoy the party, Tristan," Eve found herself saying, unable to tear her eyes away from Gabriella's gaze. "Everyone is welcome."

Gabriella extended a slim hand, which Eve took. Electric shocks coursed through her at the pressure of this beautiful girl's fingers.

"Hi, Eve," Gabriella said, in a laughing voice that felt to Eve like it was meant for her alone. "I'm very pleased to meet you."

"Gaby's here on a modelling assignment," said Tristan. He looked smug. "I'm showing her how little competition there is around here. You'd clean up around here, Gabs."

How long can a person hold eye contact before it

starts to look strange? Eve thought. She was breathless, drowning in a blue ocean. Part of her wrestled to be free of the spell that this girl had cast on her. No good could come of being attracted to anyone related to Tristan de Vere. But she couldn't help it.

Rhi was cheerfully singing "Jingle Bells" on the stage. Sensing that he had lost Eve's attention, Tristan spread his fingers and did a little comedy dance from side to side. "Ooh, 'Jingle Bells', very edgy," he remarked, grinning. "You might find this hard to believe, Gabs, but Eve organized this whole tacky winter affair. She's quite the Mother Christmas. And there was me, agog at your reputation as this town's Queen of Parties, Eve. Are you honestly telling me that this was the best you could do?"

Eve broke eye contact with Gabriella. She felt cold now, and awkward at Tristan's cruel words. It was hard to ignore the way the branches of the Christmas trees around them were already starting to wilt in the heat, showering their pine needles on the crumpled tablecloths and the scratched white floor. The disco ball screamed unoriginality. The discarded piles of Christmas jumpers, the melting heaps of fake snow, the sweaty faces of the dancers. . . She saw the marquee through Tristan's eyes and winced.

Gabriella smiled even more widely, and Eve braced herself for the joke that was guaranteed to follow. "I think it's all adorable," she said unexpectedly, looping her arm through Eve's. "You must have worked so hard to make it happen."

Tristan looked shocked. Clearly he had expected Gabriella to laugh along with him. "But Gabs," he started.

Gabriella had already started ushering Eve towards the door of the marquee. "Ignore my cousin, he's a party pooper," she said, cuddling Eve's arm a little more closely. "Do you know, when he was four he screamed the house down when Dad told him his Christmas bike was second-hand?"

Eve laughed in shock. *Gabriella has her arm through mine*, she thought, her brain whirling. *She's not laughing at me. She thinks Tristan's an idiot.*

The air was cooler outside. The lights of Heartside Bay spilled down to the harbour, a vast Christmas decoration in itself.

"Thank you," Eve managed to say. She smiled

tentatively at Gabriella. "That could have turned nasty."

"Tristan is a piece of work," Gabriella said. "A spoiled little rich boy. I think it was in his nature, right from the start. I expect he squealed when his nanny put own-brand nappies on his fat little bottom. Don't you?"

Eve laughed, then clapped her hands over her mouth. "Sorry," she said through her fingers. *Fat little bottom. . .* The thought of a bad-tempered baby Tristan was too funny.

"Laugh at my ridiculous cousin as much as you like," Gabriella said cheerfully. "I give you permission." She flicked a look at Eve through her sooty lashes. "You have a gorgeous laugh, by the way."

Eve felt the heat of Gabriella's gaze. She tried to order her muddled thoughts. She was reading this all wrong, surely. This girl – this gorgeous model – couldn't be interested in *her*.

"Show me the beach," Gabriella suggested, squeezing Eve's hand lightly. "A relaxing walk is probably just what you need after all the planning and organizing you must have done for today."

The sea breeze on the beach was a blessed relief. Eve was feeling hot all over, and not just on account of her Christmas jumper, which she realized she was still wearing. Gabriella was holding her hand, pulling her down the beach to the water's edge, talking to her, asking her questions in a constant, laughing bubble of sound.

"What made you think of this festival? It's an amazing idea, you're so talented... How did you persuade all the businesses to take part? I couldn't begin. I think you have a future as a diplomat, Eve."

Eve flushed, and stammered answers whenever Gabriella left a gap in her cheerful chatter. "I... The shopping centre was going to put local people out of business... I'm not that talented, I'm lucky because I have amazing friends..."

"Do you have someone special in your life?"

As Eve gazed into Gabriella's blue eyes, that terrible afternoon at the secret cove with Becca faded into nothing. "No, I... There was someone but ... not any more," she said. She swallowed. "She ended it."

Was she imagining it, or was there a sudden flash of delight on Gabriella's face? Tenderly, the beautiful girl reached out to brush a strand of hair out of Eve's eyes. "How could anyone dump a girl as pretty as you?" she said, her voice entirely serious.

Eve's mind was in chaos, her skin burning at the touch of Gabriella's fingers. "What about you?" she managed to ask.

Gabriella smiled a secret kind of smile. "Let's say, things just got interesting on that front."

Eve had no idea how long the two of them walked and talked, sand between their toes and the evening wind in their hair. All she knew was that this amazing girl was still holding her hand. The rest of it hardly mattered. The attraction she felt for Gabriella was instant, deep and strong. They had so much in common. It seemed extraordinary to Eve now that she had ever believed there was a future for her and Becca, with all their differences. Gabriella. . . Gabriella. . . Even her name thrilled Eve to the pit of her stomach.

Please may I not have got this wrong, she prayed, as Gabriella splashed, laughing, in the edge of the sea, beckoning Eve to join her. *Please let this girl like me. Please, please, please. . .*

EIGHTEEN

Gabriella's hair blew around her face as she splashed in the surf. "Are you coming in?" she teased. "Just a little Christmas dip?"

Eve laughed. "I can practically see the ice bobbing around in there," she said, playing along. She knew for a fact that the sea was almost at bathwater temperature, thanks to the run of hot days they'd been having.

Gabriella went into an exaggerated mime, hugging herself and shivering and whooping at the imagined cold. "Come in and keep me warm, Eve!" she shouted gleefully.

Eve could hardly speak for the longing that descended on her. The thought of putting her arms around Gabriella's beautiful slim waist, rubbing her back, feeling the black silk of her hair between her fingers. . . She bit hard on her lip, tasting blood. She wouldn't rush this. Something told her that it was way too important. Something was unfurling here – something rare, and beautiful, and strange. She wouldn't – couldn't – rush in and destroy it.

Gabriella whooped and danced in the moonlit surf like a water nymph, her hair whirling around her head. Clasping her arms around her own body as if to keep herself in check, Eve contented herself with watching.

Gabriella strode grinning out of the water. Her skin was cold and wet, but as she took Eve's hand again, the electricity that zipped through Eve was as hot as ever.

"Beautiful," said Gabriella, rubbing the back of Eve's hand with her thumb.

What's beautiful? The water, the beach, the moonlight? Me? Eve thought, with a delicious rush of excitement at the thought.

Gabriella put her arm around Eve. She was the taller of the two, and Eve fitted comfortably in the crook of her shoulder. She breathed in Gabriella's scent, feeling that long black hair tickling her face. Her stomach threatened to collapse in on itself.

"Do you want to go back to the marquee?"

I want to kiss you, Eve thought a little helplessly. She'd never felt such a strong attraction in her life. "We'd better go and see what the others are doing, I suppose," she said aloud. "Before they send out a search party."

Gabriella grinned. "Tristan's probably going bananas. Something tells me that me and you heading off together wasn't in the plan."

Eve dizzied at the thought of heading off anywhere with Gabriella. She couldn't stop thinking about the girl's beautiful mouth, or how it would feel pressed against her own. She had to get a grip.

"You know why I came tonight?" Gabriella asked as they climbed the steps up to Marine Parade and along the harbour towards the marquee. "To get to know a few people. I'm moving to Heartside Bay, you see." She smiled a blinding smile. "I can't tell you how glad I am that I came."

Eve clapped her hands to her mouth to stop herself

from screaming aloud at this news. Gabriella was moving here? "When?" she gasped.

Gabriella laughed. "Two weeks' time. Are you pleased?"

Eve knew she had the world's stupidest smile on her face, but she didn't care. She felt gloriously, ridiculously happy. She felt that, if she simply spread her arms and flapped then, she would soar into the air and swoop around the moon. Gabriella was moving here. She hardly dared to ask the question: did that mean a relationship with this incredible girl might actually happen?

"Pleased? I'm thrilled!" she managed to say.

And she felt herself falling even more deeply in love as Gabriella threw back her head and laughed in delight.

Music was still drifting out of the rose-swagged door into the great marquee, Rhi and Brody's voices intertwined.

Gabriella put her arm gently around Eve's shoulders, guiding her into the marquee. Rhi and Brody sang on.

"Gabs!" Looking put out, Tristan was striding towards them with a sulky expression on his face.

"Where have you been? I've been all by myself in this ridiculous tent—"

Gabriella turned her back on her cousin and looked into Eve's eyes. "I knew it was you," she said, stroking Eve's face with one finger. "The moment I saw you, I knew."

She cupped Eve's face and drew her close for the most electrifying kiss Eve had ever experienced. If Gabriella hadn't been holding her firmly upright, Eve knew she would have fallen over.

Tristan stopped dead, his mouth open in horror. "Gabs! What the—"

Eve stroked Gabriella's hair away from her face and kissed her back. The marquee faded to nothing. It was just her and this incredible girl, the scent of Christmas roses and pine trees, the moonlight striping the mouth of the marquee and the cool feel of Gabriella's hair entwined in her fingers. "Me too," she whispered, when at last they broke apart.

Gabriella flashed a heartbreaking smile and turned to face her apoplectic cousin. "Tristan," she said, striding into the crowd. "I wish I could say that I missed you, but I didn't."

149

Eve leaned against the marquee door, lifting her fingers to her tingling lips as Tristan chased after his cousin. A faint voice in the back of her mind was yelling at her. *This is Tristan's cousin! Don't fall in love unless you're sure, it could all be an elaborate plan he has to ruin you once and for all! You can't possibly fall for someone that fast, you've only just met her!*

"Shut up, brain," she said, and smiled at the scented white roses that hung about her like a bridal bower.

NINETEEN

Eve couldn't wipe the smile off her face for the rest of the evening. She fell asleep, hugging her pillow and smiling fit to burst, and slept for nine hours straight, dreaming of blue eyes and black hair and sweet-tasting lips. She woke up from the sweetest of dreams with her face aching. She had kissed Gabriella and Gabriella had kissed her. It was a dream come true.

Dreamily, she took a long hot shower, savouring the sting of the hot water. She rubbed conditioner through her long auburn hair, exfoliated her skin, smothered herself in body cream. Humming Christmas tunes, she applied a touch of make-up, realizing as she dusted her cheeks with her powder brush that all the mascara in the world couldn't improve the way her eyes were shining today. Choosing her favourite dress and luxuriating in the feel of the warm air on her skin after the torture of yesterday's folds of itchy wool, she slipped on her sandals and took up her bag and skipped down the stairs of the flat. She was due to meet her father for an early lunch on the waterfront, and she couldn't wait to get there.

Bring it on, world, she thought, stopping at the door to breathe the sweet summer air. *Today, I can handle anything.*

Her phone buzzed.

WHO WAS SHE? Agog doesn't cover it. TEXT ME. Lila xxx

There was one from Polly too.

Who was the pretty girl you were kissing last night?? Ollie wants to know (he's in trouble for asking!) Pxx

Eve hugged herself. She had deliberately avoided her friends after Gabriella had left, followed by her furious-looking cousin. She didn't want to share the magic of her new-found love with anyone, not yet. It was too new and wonderful. Was it even real?

You have to keep this in proportion, Eve told herself severely. *It was one night. You don't even know her surname!* But she was still smiling, even humming to herself as she walked down the High Street. The pavement felt like a cloud beneath her feet.

Everyone she passed smiled at her. Perhaps they were sensing her reckless good mood. Perhaps they were grateful for the successes of yesterday. It didn't matter. Eve smiled back, and waved at one or two of the local shop keepers chatting on the pavement in the morning sun.

This is my town, she thought happily. *Gabriella's moving to my town.* She'd never felt such a strong sense of belonging.

I'm warning you, Eve!!! #cantsleepcanteat Lila xxx

"Someone's happy," said her father, rising from the

table as Eve skipped through the door of the Ciao Café and kissed him warmly on the cheek.

"It was a good night," Eve shrugged, wanting to laugh at the bubbling secret she held in her heart. "Have you ordered?"

"I wouldn't dare," said Henry Somerstown. "You're a woman who makes her own decisions these days."

They ate two large bowls of seafood pasta between them, sharing memories of the events of the previous day. It wasn't oysters and foie gras, Eve reflected as they patted their mouths with paper napkins and washed down the lightly spiced pasta with heavy glass tumblers of iced tap water, but it was all the better for it. Those days of excess, the trips on the private jet, the fashionable restaurants and designer clothes were a long time ago now.

"On the house," said the waiter when Eve called for the bill. She recognized him as one half of a couple who'd attended yesterday's mock wedding in the marquee.

"You can't give us all this food for free," she protested.

The waiter sighed. "You're right, of course. You

haven't had any dessert." He grinned and tapped his nose. "That'll be free as well. Do you know how many bookings I've taken for Christmas already, thanks to yesterday?" He spread his arms. "The whole café, all week. I can afford two bowls of pasta for my new favourite customers."

Eve's phone buzzed. It was an email from Rhi's father.

Eve, we can't thank you enough for all your work yesterday. Please accept a permanent 15% discount on all products and services provided by the LBA in our beautiful town, with gratitude!

Patrick Wills (on behalf of the Heartside Bay LBA)

"You've really made a difference to this town, Eve," said her father, as they gratefully accepted two warm chocolate brownies and two cups of frothy coffee. "And it isn't even Christmas yet." He looked a little sad. "I feel as if you've made more difference in one day than I ever did in five years."

"The past is the past, Daddy," said Eve. Nothing was going to dim her happiness today. "Forget about it. We're all starting afresh, OK? No more recriminations, no more guilt. Just us, doing our best."

Her father took a long sip of his coffee.

"I have some news," he said as he set his cup down again. "I've been offered a good job."

Eve beamed. "That's wonderful! What are you going to be doing?"

"It's in London," he said.

For the first time that day, Eve felt jolted. "London?" she repeated in a flash of worry. "Are we going to move to London then?"

"I think Heartside Bay's had enough of me for a while," her father said wryly. "Don't you?"

Eve tried to keep the smile on her face. She didn't want to leave Heartside Bay, not not now Gabriella was about to move here. How ironic would that be? Her whole spoiled life, she'd been desperate for the bright lights of London, Paris, Milan. Heartside Bay had been small and boring, full of small and boring people. Just the way Tristan de Vere saw it. Now, everything was different.

You can't let him down now, she thought. *Mummy and Chloe have given up on him. You're all he has left. And there's no denying, we make a great team.* London wouldn't be so bad. She could visit her friends at weekends. She might even still be able to make something work with Gabriella.

"That's wonderful, Daddy," she said, trying to inject some enthusiasm into her voice. "We can make a good life for ourselves in London, I'm sure we can."

Her father reached for her hand. "I'm going alone, sweetheart," he said gently. "Your life is here, with your mother and sister."

Eve felt a small, traitorous leap of relief. She didn't have to leave. But then a strange feeling of grief settled on her instead. *I've only just got you back*, she wanted to say. *And now I'm going to lose you again?* Her eyes prickled with tears. She blinked hard.

"What . . . what's the job?" she whispered.

"I can't tell you much. But I'm going to be working for the government, in a special kind of fraud squad. I have contacts, you see. People who are of interest to the police. It's why I was released early, darling." He smiled slightly. "Your old dad is going to be a spy."

Eve felt a rush of love and sadness at his words.

"Promise me you won't tell anyone," he said, in a voice of utmost seriousness. "I shouldn't even have told you that much. There's a lot at stake, Evie. It's time I made amends. You see, I want to make a difference too."

Eve understood. *I forgive you, Daddy,* she thought, feeling a calm wash of peace settle deep in her soul at long last. *And I am proud of you too. I truly am.*

TWENTY

The strange heat of late September had finally given way to rain and cold. In some ways, it was a relief. Going to school in the blazing sun had felt wrong, as if the summer holidays had returned and no one had thought to tell the teachers.

Gabriella had sent Eve a few texts during the week, fleeting news from her busy life in London. Eve was glad they hadn't spoken. After the euphoria of Saturday night, she'd come to earth and realized how much she had to think about. Was it too early to fall for someone else? How would Becca feel, knowing she'd met someone so quickly? And the worst thought of all: were Tristan and Gabriella working together somehow, setting Eve up for a fall? She wouldn't put anything past Tristan, but she couldn't believe Gabriella would do something like that. Then again, what did she know? Blood was thicker than water.

Eve had gone out of her way to avoid Tristan all week, and her friends had done the same. He had made no attempt to seek any of them out. On good days, Eve enjoyed the sense that Tristan knew when he was beaten. On bad ones, she imagined a spider with a thousand-watt smile at the heart of a web, waiting for her to walk into his invisible trap.

She had successfully deflected her friends' questions all week. It hadn't been easy. Lila had been especially persistent, and it was only when Eve flared up at her in the canteen on Wednesday that Lila had backed off.

I'll tell you when I tell you, Eve thought to herself as she took a shower on Saturday morning. *If there's ever anything more to tell.*

There was a text from Gabriella when Eve returned from the bathroom. She snatched up her phone and read the message with her heart in her mouth.

Near Heartside today on a job. Want to come along? Gxx

The first thing Eve did was to set her phone down on her bedside table and squeal into her pillow. Then she sat back on her bed and made herself consider the risks. She lasted two seconds.

Love to. Where? Exx

I'll send a car. 20 mins? Gxx

Eve had never dried her hair so fast. Choosing what to wear these days was considerably easier than it used to be, now that she no longer had a walk-in wardrobe to get lost in. These days there were a handful of dresses, jeans, tops and cashmere jumpers. Pulling on a pale grey dress that matched her eyes, draping her neck in a butter-yellow cashmere wrap and snatching up her favourite bag, Eve was waiting on the street when the big grey car came cruising along the road to fetch her.

She'd forgotten how nice it was to be driven places. Settling back on the comfortable seats, Eve gazed out of the smoky privacy windows, trying to still her beating heart and applying a lot more lip gloss than necessary.

Within fifteen minutes, the grey car had pulled up beside the great corrugated doors of a huge warehouse. Eve climbed out to see people were hurrying back and forth with cameras slung around their necks and headphones clamped on their heads. Lighting equipment and high-vis jackets and snaking cables were everywhere.

"Quickly, please!"

Eve looked in some surprise at the large black woman beckoning her from a small fire door. "Me?"

"Give your book to my assistant, get yourself into make-up as quickly as you can." The large woman checked a slim gold watch. "You're needed approximately ten minutes ago."

Eve realized the mistake. She felt absurdly pleased. "Oh, no," she said, smiling, "I'm not a model."

The large woman's eyes widened. She looked down at the clipboard in her hand, then back at Eve again. "Are you sure?" she said doubtfully. "We're expecting another one."

This was all so surreal, Eve wanted to giggle. "I'm here to see Gabriella?"

The large woman sighed. "In you come," she said, shooing Eve inside. "Come along, quickly please, we don't have all day."

The warehouse was filled with snow. Eve had the oddest sense that she had slipped back a week, and she was back in the mocked-up Winter Wonderland.

"Move along, please," said the large woman behind her a little impatiently.

"What's the shoot?" Eve asked, gazing in some wonder at the beautiful icy pond that had been constructed in one corner of the warehouse, the snowy ski-slope in the middle and the cosy log cabin along the back wall. Every detail was perfect.

"A spread for the December issue of *Bellissima*, the fashion magazine. The photographer is surprisingly particular about timekeeping, for an Italian," said the black woman. She glared back at the warehouse door. Eve decided she wouldn't want to be in the late model's Prada shoes, whenever she chose to arrive

When Eve saw Gabriella laughing with a make-up artist at the foot of the ski-slope, her breath caught in her throat. Gabriella was wearing a slim-fitting ski-suit, her black jacket edged with fluffy fake fur. Furry boots were laced all the way up her long legs, and her hair hung in a gorgeously woven blue-black plait over one shoulder. It was unimaginable that this gorgeous, glamorous girl had kissed her last Saturday, Eve thought in a daze. How had it happened?

Gabriella caught sight of her. Breaking off her conversation, she beamed and waved a gloved hand. There was a volley of shutter sound.

"*Bella*," said the photographer, lowering his camera. Eve realized with astonishment that it was Lorenzo Mazzoli. "Now Elorina, is there any sign of Liliana?"

"Not yet," replied the black woman anxiously.

Lorenzo muttered under his breath. "Then we must wait," he said, sounding tetchy. "But not much longer, OK?" Spotting Eve, he raised his eyebrows briefly and waved, then returned to his camera. "We will take more shots by the pond, Gabriella."

"Give me a few minutes, Lorenzo." Gabriella stripped off her gloves and tossed them to a waiting assistant before breaking into a run across the warehouse. "Eve! It's so good to see you!" she cried, and she wrapped Eve up in a warm, furry hug.

Eve's first instinct was to hug Gabriella back as hard as she could, and shower kisses on her beautiful face. But something held her back. *Coming here was risk enough*, she thought. She had to talk to Gabriella, explain the way she was feeling before she could let anything else happen.

Gabriella sensed her reticence. "What's up?" she said, pulling back in surprise.

Eve swallowed. "Can we talk?"

"How about we go inside the log cabin?" Gabriella giggled. "It's so cute, wait until you see the styling. We're shooting in there next."

The cabin was a perfect replica of a tiny Alpine chalet, with a veranda and small leaded windows. A real fire was flickering in the grate. Gabriella led Eve to a big checked sofa covered in gorgeous soft woollen throws, her arm lightly around Eve's waist.

"It's like this," Eve began as Gabriella sat beside her with her long fingers laced around her knees. "You know I told you that I'd ended it with someone just the other day? Or, you know – they ended it with me?"

"Please don't tell me you've got back together with her."

Eve shook her head. "I don't know, Gabriella," she burst out, "these *feelings* . . . I really like you, but it's so soon after breaking up with Becca, my ex-girlfriend, and I know you're Tristan's cousin and we don't exactly get on and—"

Gabriella laid a cool finger tip on Eve's lips, silencing her. "Eve, I understand your fears. I've been there too. But I think you and me have real potential. I genuinely like you, and I really want a relationship with you."

Eve could feel tears filling her eyes. She so badly wanted this to be true. "But Tristan—"

"My cousin," Gabriella interrupted again, "as I think we established last week, is an idiot. I only came to the party with him because I wanted to meet a few people. I'm moving to Heartside in just a couple of weeks' time, remember? I should have known Tristan wouldn't have helped me to make the best first impression on the prettiest girl I've ever met, but he's family. Family sucks sometimes, but it's still family."

Eve stared in some disbelief at the pretty flush

stealing up Gabriella's cheeks. She realized that this gorgeous girl was as nervous as she was.

"Believe me, I know *all* about families," she said with some feeling.

Gabriella smiled. "I'd never let Tristan come between us," she said softly.

The large black woman put her head around the door, looking frazzled. "Sorry to interrupt," she said. "There's no sign of Liliana and we're at our wits' end for this double shoot on the pond, Lorenzo is about to lose his considerable temper. Can you talk to him, Gabriella?"

Gabriella's eyes gleamed. She took Eve's hand and hauled her to her feet. "I have an idea. Go and see Rico, he's the guy in charge of the outfits. Let's go skating."

"What?" Eve protested, but she let Gabriella lead her out of the door and push her towards a skinny whippet-like man with a long silver rail full of ravishing winter fashions. "Gabriella, I—"

"Dress her up, Rico," Gabriella ordered. She shot Eve a wink. "Put her in the white trousers, the blue and green gilet – yes, that one – and how about the moccasins? The trapper hat will solve at least half of the hair issues. We can deal with make-up in a minute. Rico, what are you putting me in next?"

Feeling dazed by events, Eve went behind a makeshift screen, took off her grey dress and carefully slid on the beautiful garments being thrust through the curtain at her. The white trousers fit like a second skin, and the blue cardigan with the geometric trim was stunning. Slipping her feet into the soft moccasins, she stared at herself in the mirror.

"You'll do," said Rico with a sniff. "Alice! Sort this one's hair out, will you?"

Gabriella was wearing an amazing striped red jumper and skin-tight black leggings, a geometric patterned gilet and a trapper hat similar to Eve's. She took Eve's hand and pulled her over to the ice pond, with Eve protesting most of the way.

"Gabriella, are you sure I can do this? Don't you have to ask Lorenzo first? I've never done a photo shoot, I'm not a model. . ."

"You're doing us a favour, Eve, and you look beautiful. Lorenzo will do a few test shots but I'm sure he'll love you. Now stop yapping and let Clarabel do your face," Gabriella said affectionately.

A tiny girl with a crown of golden ringlets appeared, armed with more brushes and powder puffs than Eve had seen in her life, wiping Eve's face clear of the make-up she'd applied that morning and dusting a glittery powder across her cheeks. Alice the hairstylist deftly twisted Eve's auburn hair into a fishtail plait to match Gabriella's as Clarabel applied two sweeps of colour to Eve's eyelids and dabbed her lips with a warm coral stick.

"Concentrate on me," Gabriella said ten minutes later, and smiled into her eyes. "Think how much kissing we'll do right after this shoot."

Eve felt her cheeks flush. She held tightly to Gabriella's hand and looked into her beautiful blue eyes, and started to laugh as Lorenzo took a volley of test shots. This was so utterly, wonderfully crazy.

"Liliana's here!" Elorina called from the warehouse door.

"Tell her to go away again," said Lorenzo, studying the screen on the back of his camera. "We have everything we need right here."

He showed Eve the images. Eve stared at herself and Gabriella, laughing together, eyes shining, lips parted, two beautiful girls gazing at each other as if the rest of the world didn't exist. Their chemistry leaped from the camera like a living thing.

"The perfect couple," said Lorenzo in approval. "*Molto, molto bella*. More shots I think!"

TWENTY-ONE

"Wow," said Ollie.

He was staring at Gabriella with such a far away look in his eyes that Polly gave him a shove. "Ollie," she scolded, "didn't anyone ever tell you it was rude to stare?" She smiled warmly at Gabriella. "Welcome to the gang. We've all been desperate to meet the girl who's stolen Eve's heart. Sit down, make yourself at home."

Eve felt a rush of such love for Polly that it was all she could do not to throw her arms around her and kiss her on the spot. Instead she smiled and held a little more tightly on to Gabriella's hand.

It felt so right to be introducing Gabriella to her friends here at the secret cove. Being here with everyone had already erased the bad memories of her last visit, sitting here with her heart in pieces as Becca walked out of her life. The heart's ability to heal was an amazing thing.

And Gabriella is an amazing girl, Eve thought happily.

The cove had never seemed more beautiful in Eve's eyes. The rain had let up, and the sky was a riot of colours as the sun began to settle through the clouds on its way towards the horizon. Ollie and Josh had lit a campfire between them, which blazed and spat merrily, adding more colours to the evening. Brody leaned against what Eve would forever think of as the Rock of Sadness, strumming lightly at his guitar, Rhi singing beside him.

"How do you get your hair so shiny?" said Lila, staring at Gabriella in awe.

Gabriella laughed. "Neglect, mainly," she said. "I think there's Cherokee Indian in my blood somewhere down the line. You must be Lila? Eve never told me how pretty you were."

"You are going to fit right in," Josh remarked as Lila beamed with pleasure. "I can tell. Do you mind if

I draw you?"

Gabriella looked a little startled.

"Drawing is Josh's thing," said Eve, pulling her girlfriend down to sit beside her on the checked rug Polly had thrown down on the sand. "He's unbelievably good."

"Wow," said Ollie again.

"My boyfriend tends to dribble," Polly explained. "He's bit like a Labrador that way."

Lila roared with laughter.

"I don't dribble!" Ollie protested.

"What do you call that running with the ball thing you do on the football field again?" Polly asked, with a naughty twinkle in her eye.

"Dribbling," said Ollie promptly. There was more laughter. He frowned. "Oh, funny, I see what you did there. . ."

Gabriella smiled at Eve, stroking the back of her hand with her thumb. Eve could already feel the difference between her relationship with Gabriella and the one she'd had with Becca. *Everyone always says you'll know when you meet the one*, she thought, smiling back. *Now, finally, I understand.*

She liked everything about Gabriella. The way she moved, the way she brushed her hair back from her face. How her eyes changed colour with the light, the way she frowned and smiled in quick succession – the way she looked at Eve like she was the only girl in the world. Their connection was fierce and fiery, but somehow comfortable too.

"Marshmallow?" said Ollie, pulling a gooey twig from the fire and waving it under Lila's nose.

"Get that thing away from me," Lila groaned. "I feel like I've got a marshmallow baby. I'm never eating another marshmallow again."

"It's a pink one," Ollie said, waving it under her nose again.

"Oh, right," said Lila, sitting up. "Well, if it's a pink one, that's a different matter."

Josh stroked the back of Lila's head affectionately as she pulled the sticky pink goo off the twig with her teeth. "Such manners, such refinement," he said. "It quite brings tears to my eyes."

"I'll bring tears to your eyes in a minute," Lila threatened jokingly, pushing Josh backwards on to the sand so that his hat fell off and rolled towards the sea.

"Mmm," she said, smearing her sticky lips over Josh's cheek as he protested loudly, "marshmallow kisses are the best. . ."

"Marshmallow kisses," Rhi hummed. "That's a great title for a song. Brody, what do you think? The rhythm could work really well."

As Brody obligingly picked out a few chords so Rhi could start building a song, Eve picked up the sketchpad Josh had dropped. Josh had captured Gabriella's cheekbones and long straight hair to perfection, as she'd known he would.

"That's incredible," said Gabriella, gazing at the picture in astonishment. "You have really talented friends."

"I think you mean, really sticky ones," Eve said, laughing.

"Seriously, Eve," Gabriella repeated. She looked around the chattering, laughing group. "They all seem wonderful."

Eve looked at her friends. Rhi and Brody had their heads together, testing different harmonic combinations with Brody's guitar by the firelight. It was a shame they weren't a romantic item any more, but Eve was inexpressibly glad they still made music together. Ollie and Polly sat cuddling by the firelight. Eve remembered how once she'd dreamed of having Ollie for herself. The idea was ludicrous to her now. And Polly . . . she'd been through hell, but somehow come out the other side, stronger than ever.

Josh and Lila had moved on from their marshmallow kisses and were now pouring sand on the sticky smudges that remained while laughing themselves sick. It was funny to think of Josh in the old days, the nerdy mystery man always on the edge of everything who was now so firmly a part of the gang. And Lila. . . had she really only come to Heartside Bay in February? She was such a crucial member of their group, it was hard to imagine life without her.

There was a lump in Eve's throat that she couldn't put down to marshmallows. "I guess they are pretty wonderful," she said honestly. "I'm lucky to have them."

Ollie stretched and burped loudly.

"Well," Eve amended as the others groaned and waved their hands in front of their noses and Polly shrieked with disgust, "*most* of them, anyway."

"Ready to give it a go?" Rhi asked Brody. She smiled

shyly at everyone. "This is a rough draft, guys, but here goes. *Marshmallow kisses, sticky sweet surprise, hold me and kiss me with love in your eyes. . .*"

It was a sweet tune that summed up so much about the summer. Eve rested her head against Gabriella's shoulder and listened, her eyes on the setting sun. Her heart felt full.

"We should do this every year," she said as the cheering died down and Brody and Rhi bowed and grinned.

"Write songs?" said Rhi, laughing. "Fine by me."

"No. Have a beach party." Eve looked around the group. "We could make it a tradition. Wherever we are, whatever we're doing – we all come to the cove on this date. Every year, OK? No excuses."

Ollie and Josh exchanged high fives.

"Don't you have to seal a promise like that?" Lila asked through a mouthful of marshmallow.

Eve's eyes flicked to the curling surf, golden in the setting sun. "You took the words right out of my mouth," she said. She hauled Gabriella to her feet with one hand and Lila with the other. "Start running. Last one in the water is a loser!"

"Right behind you!" Ollie shouted, lifting Polly into his arms.

Lila screamed with laughter, doing her best to keep up with Eve and Gabriella as they ran at full tilt towards the shoreline. Rhi and Brody ran beside them, arms flung out wide. Eve was the first in, feeling the dash of spray on her skin like a baptism of ice. As she gasped and pulled Gabriella and a still screaming Lila with her, she spotted a lone straw item bobbing on the edge of the shore, lifting and falling with the dipping waves.

"My hat!" Josh roared, last to leap in. "*Somebody, save my hat!*"

LOOK OUT FOR MORE

HEARTSIDE BAY

Life, love and everything in between

HEARTSIDE BAY

The New Girl

CATHY COLE

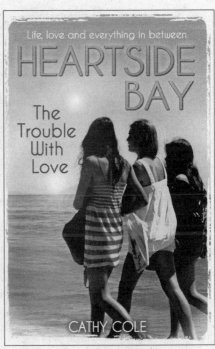

Life, love and everything in between

HEARTSIDE BAY

The Trouble With Love

CATHY COLE

Life, love and everything in between

HEARTSIDE BAY

More
Than a
Love
Song

CATHY COLE

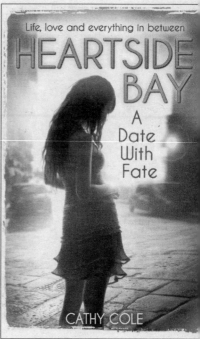

Life, love and everything in between

HEARTSIDE BAY

A
Date
With
Fate

CATHY COLE

Life, love and everything in between

HEARTSIDE BAY

Never
a Perfect
Moment

CATHY COLE

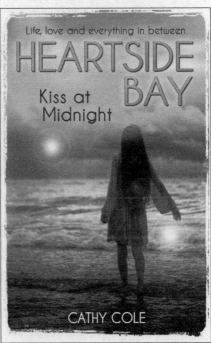

Life, love and everything in between

HEARTSIDE BAY

Kiss at
Midnight

CATHY COLE

Life, love and everything in between

HEARTSIDE BAY

Back to You

CATHY COLE

Life, love and everything in between

HEARTSIDE BAY

Summer of Secrets

CATHY COLE

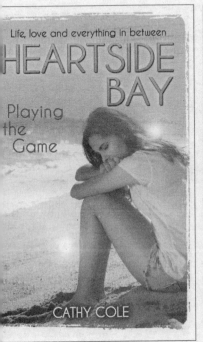

Life, love and everything in between

HEARTSIDE BAY

Playing
the
Game

CATHY COLE

Life, love and everything in between

HEARTSIDE BAY

Flirting
With
Danger

CATHY COLE

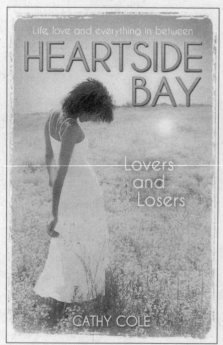

Life, love and everything in between

HEARTSIDE BAY

Lovers
and
Losers

CATHY COLE

Life, love and everything in between

HEARTSIDE BAY

Winter
Wonderland

CATHY COLE